FIRE
IN
THE
STREETS

IN

THE

kekla magoon

NEW YORK

LONDON

TORONTO

SYDNEY

NEW DELHI

ALADDIN

also by kekla magoon

THE ROCK AND THE RIVER

ALA Best Books for Young Adults
ALA Coretta Scott King/John Steptoe Award for New Talent
ALA Notable Children's Books
Bank Street Best Children's Books of the Year
Capitol Choices List (DC)
CCBC Choices (Cooperative Children's Book Council)

CAMO GIRL

ALADDIN

An imprint of Simon & Schuster Children's Publishing Division

1230 Avenue of the Americas, New York, NY 10020

First Aladdin hardcover edition August 2012

Copyright © 2012 by Kekla Magoon

All rights reserved, including the right of reproduction in whole or in part in any form.

ALADDIN is a trademark of Simon & Schuster, Inc., and related logo is a registered trademark of Simon & Schuster, Inc.

For information about special discounts for bulk purchases, please contact Simon & Schuster Special Sales at 1-866-506-1949 or business@simonandschuster.com.

The Simon & Schuster Speakers Bureau can bring authors to your live event. For more information or to book an event contact the Simon & Schuster Speakers Bureau at 1-866-248-3049 or visit our website at www.simonspeakers.com.

Designed by Karin Paprocki

The text of this book was set in Cochin.

Manufactured in the United States of America 0712 FFG

2 4 6 8 10 9 7 5 3 1

Library of Congress Cataloging-in-Publication Data

Magoon, Kekla.

Fire in the streets / by Kekla Magoon. — 1st Aladdin hardcover ed.

p. cm.

Sequel to: The rock and the river.

ISBN 978-1-4424-2230-8

[1. Civil rights movements—Fiction. 2. Black Panther Party—Fiction. 3. Brothers and sisters—Fiction. 4. Racism—Fiction. 5. African Americans—Fiction. 6. Chicago (Ill.)—History—20th century—Fiction. 7. United States—History—20th century—Fiction.] I. Title.

PZ7.M2739Fir 2012

[Fic]—dc23

2011039129

ISBN 978-1-4424-2232-2 (eBook)

for
PAM H.

CHAPTER 1

BAD THINGS HAPPEN IN THE HEAT, THEY say. It's headed to be a scorcher. Dawn just barely cracking, sweat sheen already on the skin. Today could turn into a lot of things, but when it's hot like this, ain't none of them good.

There's a knot in my stomach the size of my fist. No, bigger. Today's the sort of day when it's best to lay low, and that's not what we're doing.

Hamlin steers the old pickup through the Chicago streets real slow, headed toward the demonstration downtown. Squeezed up next to him in the cab, me and Emmalee and Patrice sit silent. We squint through the windshield into the sun rising over the lake.

It's strange, the three of us being together like this but not saying nothing. Patrice knows how to work her mouth, and I can give her a run for her money. Emmalee always gets her word in too, no question. From the time we meet up every morning till we get to school or the Panther office, wherever. Jawing. And here we sit all wide-eyed dumb like strangers.

Then again, we're usually alone. Right now Hamlin's sitting so close his elbow bangs into me with every turn of the wheel.

"Sorry, Maxie."

"It's okay." But I hold my arms crossed over my chest to keep him from hitting anything private.

In the back, perched among the boxes, is Raheem and the kid we all call Gumbo, real name: George. He came up from the way South some time ago and his voice holds that certain twang. Nice enough guy, decent-looking. People mostly say the same about Raheem, but seeing as he's my brother, I can't really judge. He's back there and probably looking over my shoulder, as usual. Maybe even wishing he hadn't let me come along.

Raheem's always saying how he's responsible for me, which means he won't let me do anything that counts and he says "Maxie, when you're older" as the answer to just about everything. Raheem's a Black Panther already, and I'm going to be one too, just as soon as they let me. Fourteen's not old enough, apparently.

Hamlin bends over the steering wheel as the truck curves through the Loop. He's vigilant, studying our surroundings like he's taking the temperature of things, as we get closer to the park. Block after block, the city comes awake—store windows snap open, people ease along the sidewalks, sip coffee, buy newspapers.

Today's headlines should have been enough to scare us into staying home, with all their talk of police riots at the demonstration last night. Now everything seems calm and quiet. Like a regular Tuesday morning. Except for the police vehicles lining the streets, many more than I've ever seen at once.

Emmalee yawns, breaking the stillness. Cuts a sideways glance toward me. Beyond her, Patrice is chewing on her nails, the only one of us not even trying to hide her nervousness. I breathe out long and slow, trying to settle the knot in my belly. I got us into this, and we don't even know yet what *this* really is.

I'm not usually scared to go to a demonstration, but Raheem says this one won't be like any demonstration we've ever been to. He tried to warn me off coming, but I have to be there. The Democratic National Convention is the biggest thing to happen in Chicago since . . . I don't know what, and if there's going to be a demonstration and the Panthers are going to be there, then I'm going to be there too. I told him, plain as day.

The girls came along because we go everywhere together.

Around the neighborhood people run our names together like one word: "Hey, MaxiePatriceEmmalee." Inseparable. Close like sisters, for as long as I can remember. Through good times, sad times, crazy times. Right now qualifies as a downright rough time. The world is shifting—exploding, really—and none of us knows how to deal with it.

At least once a week, Emmalee still breaks down crying over Dr. King being killed, even though it happened nearly five months ago. She carries this book of his writings in her backpack like a Bible, all the pages folded down. We tried to tell her, if you fold down *all* the pages, what's the point? But then she only cries harder. Patrice is matter-of-fact about it, thinks everything's going to work out in the end, which is so far the opposite of me that sometimes we end up spitting, fighting mad at each other.

When I told the girls I wanted to join the Black Panthers, Patrice called me a hothead. Emmalee was excited but scared. They don't know what joining entirely means and neither do I, but I know the Panthers are going to change everything and we have to be a part of it. When we go down to the community center on Wednesdays to hear Leroy Jackson speak, he makes me feel like things are finally going to get better. The Panthers are going to make it so that we never have to worry about being hungry, or losing our apartment, or getting arrested for no good reason.

When Leroy throws his fist up in the air and shouts *"All power to the people!"* there's this energy that rises up around me that's like nothing I've ever felt before.

I tighten my fists in my lap. Maybe if I clench hard enough, I'll start to feel powerful inside, instead of scared.

Emmalee sighs, leans her head against mine. She spreads her hand across my knotted knuckles. Her gentle fingers clutch mine, tight and trembling. I know she's scared, probably more than me. I wouldn't have made them come with me, but they've always got my back. That's how it is with us.

Hamlin turns a corner, and suddenly the road ahead is clogged with cars. The vague echo of many voices chanting begins to reach us. I can sense the rhythm of the chant but can't quite make out the words. It doesn't sound familiar. Nothing about today feels familiar. This is an anti-war protest, Raheem told me, not a civil rights demonstration like we're used to. Most of the people there will be white. I try to pretend we're heading toward any old protest, but it's no longer so easy to pretend because I can see them weaving among the cars. White face after white face, all tensed up and in a hurry. Traffic is practically stalled letting them pass.

Hamlin hums quietly for a while, which covers us in some kind of spell. Safe enough. I don't mind the closeness in the cab. All pressed together like this, nothing can get to us. For a while. Then Hamlin stops humming, taps the wheel twice with his thumb, and the world beyond our little pocket merges closer.

The protestors seem to be coming from everywhere, out of buildings and alleys and some of the cars, carrying things and climbing over whatever's in the way. A girl with white-blond hair and dirt-smudged skin edges around our front bumper, holding hands with a guy who has a thick bandage of white gauze taped to the side of his face. He stumbles, and she steadies him. Then they move on, away.

I glance across the cab at my friends, knowing it isn't the time of day or Hamlin either that's got our tongues tied. There's something in the air. Heavier than heat and thicker than humidity. A feeling like we're rolling into trouble.

C H A P T E R 2

THE TRUCK INCHES ALONG. EVERY SQUEAK of the worn brakes sounds like seagulls. Hamlin's trying to get us close to the park, but the traffic is something else. Roads closed and cars sent around the long way to make room for the protesters flocking toward the park. We watch them squeezing among the cars to get to where they're going, dragging their signs and flyers and friends and tripping along their way. They form a fast-rushing stream that seems neverending, a thousand faces like so many white-capped waves.

I start to worry about what'll happen when we get out of the car, because it's just the six of us right now. Will we be swept into the flow, and drown?

Hamlin thumps the steering wheel, mutters something that sounds like "Is this even worth it?"

But it's already been decided. I was in the Panther office last week when Leroy Jackson and some other guys were arguing about whether or not the Panthers should have a presence at the Democratic National Convention.

"There's no place for us there."

"We gotta take a stand against the war."

"It's a white protest. They don't care about us at all."

"We need all the allies we can get."

Leroy, who's in charge, decided that it would be worth sending people to the protest, partly to sell copies of *The Black Panther*, our community newspaper, but mainly just to be a presence in the crowd. I really hope the others get here soon.

"We'll be okay," I say out loud. Maybe I'm answering Hamlin. Maybe I'm reassuring the girls. Emmalee's fingers still grip my locked fist.

Hamlin glances at us. "Yeah. Just stick together," he says. "No matter what happens."

"We will." He doesn't need to tell us. It's how we survive.

I'm still amazed that the girls and I are being allowed to come along. We're assigned to help Hamlin and the guys set up, and then we're supposed to leave, but I'm planning to stay as long as possible. At least long enough to hear Bobby Seale speak.

"What time does Bobby come onstage?" I ask. Now that the silence is broken, it's going to be hard for me to keep my mouth shut. Talking stops me from thinking, and when my thoughts are all about how I hope I don't die today, that's probably a good thing.

"Sometime this afternoon," Hamlin answers. "He's flying in from Oakland now."

Emmalee stirs a little. She wants to meet Bobby too, I know. She likes reading his writings, almost as much as she likes reading Huey's. Huey Newton and Bobby Seale are the Black Panther Party founders. Huey is the Panthers' minister of defense and Bobby's the general chairman of the party, which was started in Oakland, California, but stretches across the whole country now.

"Is Bobby coming to the office later too? I can't wait to see him in person," I blurt. "I want to hear him speak up close. It's so exciting."

"Yeah," Hamlin says. He's all cool about it because he's met Bobby in person lots of times. Hamlin had been out in Oakland for the past few months, learning about how the Panthers operate out there, and came back to help get the Chicago chapter up and running smoothly. So far, so good.

"How much farther?" I ask. The truck has moved less than half a block in the whole time we've been talking.

"I don't know," Hamlin says. "Might be as close as we're gonna get."

Raheem knocks on the back window. "We can hoof it from here," he calls. "This is taking forever."

Hamlin tosses him a thumbs-up and begins a several-minutes-long ease over to the right-hand side of the street.

We're closer to the center of things now. Through the gaps between the buildings, the crowd teems. From our slight distance their heads bob in a small swirling mass. The chanting and roaring rolls toward us in waves. Up close will be . . . I still don't know what it'll be like, just that I have some wrong feeling about it all.

"Okay, girls," Hamlin says as the tires skim the curb.

Patrice levers open the door and we pile out onto the sidewalk. We stand at the edge while Raheem and Gumbo unload the boxes, pausing every couple of minutes to let Hamlin roll the truck forward with traffic. Raheem stands in the back handing boxes down and Gumbo's on the street with us, stacking them on the hand truck they borrowed from someone's job.

When the hand truck is full, what's left in the pickup's bed are some loose bags and the Black Panther Party banner we'll be carrying. Raheem starts handing things to us.

Emmalee slings all the cloth bags over her shoulders. She looks like a horse with saddlebags out of some cowboy picture. Patrice and I kind of laugh.

"What?" she says.

"Nothing." Patrice grins, all sweet and innocent. Emmalee narrows her eyes, not a bit fooled. We've been friends too long for any kind of wool to be pulled.

"Neigh. Neeeeeigh." I paw the ground with my toe. Patrice busts up. Emmalee glares.

Then Raheem hands down the tall poles we're gonna use to hang up the banner. Patrice takes them in her hands, straightens up, and turns real serious all of a sudden. It's like —*zap*—called up for duty.

Emmalee gets in on the joke. "Spear carrier," she whispers. Patrice's mouth twitches, but she holds the smile off, makes a fierce warrior face instead.

"Aieee." She pounds the poles on the ground.

Laughing lets the nervous ache in my stomach ease up for a second. Maybe we all feel the same, 'cause for a minute we get to grinning.

Raheem jumps down from the truck bed and dumps the banner into my arms. It's heavier than I expected. I clutch it tight, nearly bending forward under the weight of it, and wait for the girls to make a joke on me. But they're staring at something behind me, and they aren't smiling anymore.

A clump of policemen—six, no, eight—marches along the sidewalk, right toward us. They're half a block away, but their presence pushes out around them like a cloud. Clad in their pale blue shirts with helmets to match. Batons dangling from their belts like little warning flags.

fireinthestreets

CHAPTER 3

THE POLICE BRUSH BY US WITHOUT STOP-
ping. Seeing them gives me a chill, all the same.
I try to shake the cold feeling, to get brave
inside, but I can't. Where there are cops,
there's trouble. Never fails.

Just last week, a pair of cops blipped their siren at us for
crossing on the red. Jumped out of the car and started yelling. Came over to us. We stood shaking in the crosswalk,
thought we were goners for sure. But they just shouted
awhile. Laughed at Emmalee's "pickaninny tears." That's
what they called it.

I see cops, and I can't help but think about the worse
things too. My friend Bucky getting beat with a baton on
the street right in front of me. That was six months ago, but
I still wake up some mornings thinking about how broken
they made him look. How small.

Senseless things. Once, when I was little, Raheem was

walking me home from school and he was doing this airplane thing with his arms to make me laugh. Raheem was little, too—maybe eleven—but already kind of tall, with long arms, which was why it was funny watching him zoom around. He tripped on a sidewalk crack and stumbled, caught his balance by leaning his hands and belly against the side of a parked sedan. Cop came up out of nowhere, accused Raheem of trying to steal the car. Got the handcuffs out and everything. A white man came out of a store just then. Didn't even say nothing, but didn't move along, either. He stood there watching, and the cop backed off. I didn't recognize the white man, didn't know what he was doing down in the neighborhood, but now I know him being there, seeing it, might have been all that saved Raheem from getting scooped up. Act of God or something. After the cop left, Raheem picked me up and hugged me and made me promise never to tell anyone. He acted like it was a one-time thing, a secret. But I learned the lesson good that day: In the neighborhood, you always got to be on your toes.

When the cops are past, when the moment is over, I look toward Raheem. Feeling glad he's here today, which is all that matters. Today. Like he says sometimes—there's a lot of "what if" in our lives; doesn't do any good to dwell on it.

"We'll go down to the corner and wait for you," Raheem says through the truck window.

Hamlin shakes his head. "Don't wait. No idea how long I'll be."

"Look for us by the stage." Raheem slaps the open window. "Hopefully we can get the banner up quick. That'll help."

We start moving toward the demonstration. "Pigs are out in force," Gumbo murmurs as we walk.

He's right. Cops everywhere, lining the edges of the park around where the protesters have begun to gather. Seeing them in their straight, cold, black-and-blue rows — the only familiar sight before me — sends a shiver across my back. We'll have to cross through in order to join the protesters behind them. Usually, behind the police is the place I *want* to get to, but nothing back there seems comforting. I can't see a single hint of brown skin anywhere, except ours.

Emmalee works her fingers into the crook of my arm and pulls closer. I figure she's thinking the same thing as me, that we've never seen so many white faces all in one place before. Except maybe from a distance, or maybe on TV. Leroy promised us the people in the crowd are our allies, but it still feels strange walking into them.

We shift toward a gap in the police barricades. The officers are lined up in double rows. I look at the crowd, and I look at the stern-faced cops. I don't understand why there are so many, because everyone here is white. It makes me scared, scared that they've been waiting for us.

I feel all their eyes on us as we get closer. Little round helmets. Chubby cheeks. *Pigs*, I think, trying to calm myself down. It doesn't really work.

A rippling banner posted high on one of the buildings says: WELCOME, DEMOCRATIC NATIONAL CONVENTION DELE-GATES. It's signed by Richard J. Daley, the mayor of Chicago. King of the pigs, Raheem would say.

As if he knows what I'm thinking, Raheem chuckles low. The it's-not-really-funny kind of laugh. "Pigs on parade. Dick Daley done himself proud."

"Shh." I don't want anyone to hear him. The police are all on Daley's side. If the mayor orders them to kill us, they will. He's tried it before.

Raheem cuts his gaze down to me. "Hey. You remember what I told you?"

"I remember."

At home this morning, Raheem had made me promise that whatever happened, the girls and me wouldn't stay in the park after dark. He'd said it first thing when he woke me up, right into my face, like he already knew I was going to defy him and stay past when we were supposed to.

"I want to hear Bobby," I told him.

"That's still daylight. You leave right after," he said. "Promise me."

"I promise."

"There's pigs all over that joint," he added. "Stuff tends to happen when the sun goes down."

Rumors travel fast, breathed from one person to another like germs. There'd been trouble in the park last night, and everyone was already on edge.

I sucked my teeth at him. "Whoever heard of a white-people riot?"

Raheem looked at me slantwise. "These cats shake it up," he said. "Remember Columbia? They tried to take over the damn college."

"Yeah."

"They be stunting things we couldn't get away with in a million years."

I shrugged. "We're going to their demonstration for a reason. We all want the same things."

"They're protesting a war abroad; we're fighting a war right here. They're trying to keep out of uniform; we're already on the front lines."

He held my shoulders. "Listen. Don't let nobody white talk you into doing nothing. You hear me? They got no fear. When the law comes down, it comes down on us."

I don't like the feeling it gives me, thinking about that.

"Maxie." Patrice huddles close to me. "What are we doing here?" She's clutching the banner poles so tight her knuckles are pale.

"Shh," I whisper. "It's going to be okay." Even though I'm not so sure of that myself.

Patrice glances over her shoulder, releases a tiny, desperate sigh. I don't have to look to know. The edge of the crowd is somewhere far behind us. We've disappeared into the middle. Nothing but people, pressed close and jumping, rocking, chanting. I'm surrounded by the chests and shoulders of people taller than me, trying to forge a path through them. All I see are vests and beads, jeans and belts, cutoff shirtsleeves, scruffy beards. Lots of long, straight hair. All I can breathe is the scent of people sweating, the occasional sweet whiff of smoke.

"Excuse us," I call out.

A large blond man looks down at me. Clear blue eyes, like surface of a pool. His gaze catches mine, makes me nervous. Then he steps aside an inch, which is about all he has to offer.

"Thanks." I barely breathe the word. Shove Patrice through the small opening first and drag Emmalee through behind me. Our feet tangle with the thick layers of paper and trash littering the ground.

fireinthestreets

17

Raheem steers us toward a thin spot in the crowd, as close to the stage as we can get. "Let's set up here," he says, kicking aside some discarded food sacks to make room for our boxes.

Emmalee sets down her bags and starts unfolding the banner from my arms. Patrice struggles to angle the poles down without hitting anyone.

"Watch out," Gumbo says. "We'll do it."

"We can help," I say, but he lifts the banner from my arms, letting it loop toward the ground. Raheem leaves an opened box and takes the poles from Patrice.

My arms have been sweating under the thick fabric. The sudden breeze on my skin is refreshing, but leaves me with a bit of a chill. Now there's nothing at all between me and the crowd. I can feel them jostling, feel them breathing. They smell strange, sound strange. Their energy is all up in the air above us, slightly floating, slightly pressing down.

The guys are tall enough to heft the banner onto the poles. They tug on it and the fabric snaps tautly into place. It reads THE BLACK PANTHER PARTY with the sprawling cat logo underneath.

They twist and twist until the poles sink into the grass, still dewy with morning mist.

"That'll do," Gumbo says.

"Now what?" Patrice is nervous. She keeps shifting her

hand from one hip to the other, like she does on test days at school.

"Stand by the pole," Raheem says. "Don't let anyone knock it over."

"That's it?" Emmalee says. "We came all this way to stand by a pole?"

Raheem shrugs. "Someone's got to do it. It's better than having to hold it up all day."

"Not much," I say. But we do it. We form a little triangle around the pole on Gumbo's end, our backs to it, with our shoulders touching on each side. Patrice takes my hand, so I take Emmalee's too. The three of us together, facing the world. It should be okay, as long as we have each other.

But when I look around, all I feel is surrounded.

CHAPTER 4

THE SUN IS BEATING LIKE SOME KIND OF cruel oven. Trying to cook us, trying to sweat us out. Every crease of my body is damp. I open my elbows over and over, trying to feel a breeze. The air is thick and still.

A man I used to know, one of Mama's, always called these the dog days. Don't know what it ever meant, but it feels true. Working like a dog. Sweating like a dog. No kinda choice about nothing, like a dog.

We've been standing by the pole all morning. Watching the guys move around us, hawking the paper and talking to people in the crowd. Now they've drifted away, closer to the stage, leaving us unprotected.

The protesters are screaming, chanting, shaking their signs. *"Hey, hey, LBJ—How many kids did you kill today?"* There's nothing good in the tone of things. Their spitting, hissing rage spills out over everything. Every bit of their movement leaves me feeling further and further away. There's a feeling in the air that wants into me, but I'm holding it at bay.

I try to hold myself above it, and I start to feel like I'm floating. Floating on a sea of white faces and colorful signs. I try to read them as they bump along over the heads of the crowd.

The big HHH stands for Hubert Horatio Humphrey, vice president of the United States, trying to move up a slot in the next election. Many more signs bear the huge face of Gene McCarthy, another candidate. The McCarthy fans seem to be everywhere. Half the time they're just shouting his name. *"Mc-Car-thy! Mc-Car-thy!"*

Plenty of posters scream END THE WAR IN VIETNAM. Because that's what everyone wants. Everyone except the Washington dogs, Raheem says. Our cousins went over. One of them died. Lots of brothers from the neighborhood too. Some we liked, some we didn't, but in the end it was all-around bad no matter what the score was personally. It scares me to think that Raheem could be next. He turns eighteen in a couple of weeks. His name will go into the draft, and if his number comes up he'll have to go fight. I can barely allow myself to imagine how that would feel.

The protesters bob and sway. I float. "Peace now, peace

forever!" some guy shouts. The chant swells and crashes like a wave against rocks.

I start to feel an itch under my skin. It makes me want to move, to grab a sign and start screaming to match the energy around me. I eye the box of newspapers sitting open beside us. We aren't supposed to be selling the paper ourselves—that's a job reserved for the older, full-on Panthers—but we're the only ones near the banner right now, and the papers are just sitting there.

I pull one out of the box and set it on top to serve as a display. People want to see what they're buying. I'd be a good saleswoman, I know. Better than some of the stiffs I've seen trying to hawk the paper around the neighborhood. I'm good at math—not like you really need to be to hold on to a bunch of quarters—plus, no one knows *The Black Panther* better than me. I've seen every issue of the paper since they first started coming around in Chicago. I've studied all the pictures and looked at every article. Even though I had to let Emmalee read out loud to me when the letters moved on the page, I remember every word. I even bought copies of three different issues myself, when there were poems published that I liked best and I could get the twenty-five cents together.

I pull another copy from the box and hold it up. *"The Black Panther* community newspaper, twenty-five cents. Get your *Black Panther* here," I call out.

"Maxie," Patrice hisses. "What are you doing?"

"It's okay," I tell her. She looks worried anyway. People get arrested when they're selling sometimes. It's not illegal, but it's one of the ways the cops like to bother us.

"Don't," Patrice says. "You'll get us in trouble." I'm not sure if she means in trouble with the Panthers or the cops, but I'm not worried. The guys have been selling all morning, and nothing's happened.

"*The Black Panther*," I say.

"Maxie!" Emmalee eyes the crowd. "Be careful. You never know who's a cop." A little while ago, Hamlin came by and warned us that there might be plainclothes officers hiding in the crowd. Local cops or even the FBI. Keeping an eye on things . . . and people.

"Get your *Black Panther* here," I call again. No one really seems to notice. They're too busy chanting and cheering.

The convention is all about who's going to be picked to run for president. Raheem says it's six one way, half a dozen the other, which basically means it doesn't matter much. A white president is a white president and none of them would really look out for black folk after the voting is done. The only one we had any hope about was Robert F. Kennedy, but someone shot him dead right when it looked like he might go all the way to the White House.

Dr. King, dead. RFK, dead. It gets to be too much

fireinthestreets

23

sometimes, hoping after things that keep getting snatched away. I don't know if the war is ever going to end, the one that's far away or the one that's here and up close. All I know is, I'm going to be part of the fight.

"*The Black Panther* community newspaper," I call into the crowd.

Their screaming swells louder, a great surge of voices. Something's happened. I can't see far enough to know exactly what. My heart beats hard, but I don't let myself be scared. I'm going to be a Panther soon, and Panthers don't get scared. Panthers always stand up.

I notice several other Panthers approaching. They've started to arrive. Black berets bobbing among the crowd. Sweat sheen on their skin, like mine. Like everyone's. I'm glad to see them out there. Nothing can touch us, as long as they're nearby.

"I want to go home," Patrice says. "Let's go."

"No," I say. "We're not done." There are papers to sell, things to see. And usually when I hang around long enough, someone sees me and puts me to work.

Emmalee's on my side. "This is weird, but kind of neat," she says, eyes wide as anything. "We should stay."

We have to stay. Bobby Seale's coming. It's not the only reason to stay, but I can't put my finger on the other thing.

o   o   o

The heat of the day grows thicker, and the crowd near the stage thins somewhat as people shift in and out of their places. A lull falls over things, a respite from the shouting voices coming out of the stage speakers. After hours of it, their words are a blur, variations on "End the war" and "Vote McCarthy." When the speakers hum, empty, for the first time all day I feel like I can actually breathe.

Two blond girls in flowing skirts go running by me. The skirts stir the air around my display copy of the paper and send its pages floating to the ground.

I crouch down to scoop them up, and suddenly my hands aren't the only ones reaching to straighten the mess. Boy hands. Hands I know. I follow the line of the leather jacket sleeve, up his shoulders to his face.

"Sam."

"Hi," he says, handing me the loose papers.

We stand up, and to avoid looking at him I make a point of lining the pages up all neat on the box top and picking off the blades of grass that linger.

"Hi." I don't know what to make of his sudden appearance. Things haven't been good for a while now. To get into it all again . . . just the thought makes me tired. "What do you want?"

Sam rolls his shoulders around inside his jacket. It still

hangs too wide and heavy on his shoulders, and it must be ridiculously hot. But it's Steve's jacket. I haven't seen Sam without it in all the three months since Steve, his brother, got shot and died. It has a dark X of tape patching the hole where one of the bullets went through it. Morbid, it seems to me. I don't like to see Sam in it. It gets between us in a way, a leather wall I don't want to get close to, can't ever cross. Sam hides behind it, just the same, and I guess that's what went wrong with us.

"Leroy sent me."

Relief. Disappointment. They hit at the same time. I cross my arms. "And?"

"He wants you and the girls to come over to the stage."

"Now? What for?" We'd have to leave the banner unattended.

"He's going to speak soon and he wants more folks on hand to sell the paper."

"Fine, we'll come now. Why'd he send you?" I give him the look that says we're over, just in case one of us needs reminding. I catch occasional glimpses of the stage area from here; maybe a dozen Panthers mill around there. Figures, out of all of them, Leroy would pick my ex-boyfriend to carry his message.

Sam rolls his shoulders again. "Leroy always thinks he knows best, right?"

"Tell him to mind his own business." I say it kind of snotty. Leroy's second only to Fred Hampton as Chicago chapter leader, so I wouldn't have said anything of the kind to his face, but Sam needs to know where I stand with things.

"I can help you with the papers," he says, grabbing for a box still full of newspapers.

"Fine, since you're going anyway. I'll get the girls and meet you over there."

Never mind that Emmalee and Patrice are standing five feet from us. But they're looking every which way and acting right, like they haven't heard everything we've been saying.

"I guess so," Sam says. "See you."

As he backs away, I can see it in his eyes, the way he's drifting. I will myself not to care.

C H A P T E R 5

UT FROM UNDER THE PANTHER BAN-
ner, everything feels different. We cluster
together, an armful of papers each. I wish
we had the Panther jackets, or at least the
berets, to let people know we aren't just here on our own.
We squeeze on through, but without the larger guys and
the bulky stuff to force a path for us it's harder. Emmalee
is cute and polite so we put her to go through first, but
more than once someone does a bit of a double take and
frowns, the way you might look at a stain on a nice clean
tablecloth when you're not sure how it got there. A girl my
own height shrugs away as I slide past her, like she doesn't
want my skin to touch hers. I want to tell her that black
don't rub off, but by the time I blurt it out, she's already
found some distance from me. Patrice smacks my arm, and
I know it means watch your mouth. It's always been kind
of a problem.

Leroy's already speaking before we get close enough to see him. His voice echoes out over the crowd.

"The Black Panther Party stands in solidarity with the anti-war movement," he's saying. "Will you stand with us in return? We are fighting a war here in our own land. In our own black communities. A fight that is being waged by black citizens and white citizens alike in this nationwide movement for civil rights."

When we get through the thick of things, I see some Panthers down front, trying to energize the crowd, though Leroy can manage it all on his own. He has a way with words, which is how he ended up in charge.

"We believe America can be better than what it has become," he says. "One hundred years out of slavery and we are still colonized. Nearly two hundred years since the Declaration of Independence, and we are still not free."

The speakers boom and tremble, as if they feel Leroy's conviction. "We have been to Selma, and Montgomery, and Birmingham, and Oakland. We have marched for equality under the banner of unconditional peace, yet at our every turn we have been met with crushing, irrevocable acts of violence."

We stop pushing through the crowd, because we simply want to listen. Will the white demonstrators come to our side? Will they become the allies Leroy hopes they can be? It occurs to me that if not, we will truly be surrounded.

"When peace-loving citizens are unjustly and brutally murdered by the police—agents of the very government that is supposed to protect us—when we are slaughtered in the streets out of hatred or fear, such actions are low. Dirty. These are the actions of pigs. We call these corrupt officers pigs when they act as pigs."

Here we are, entirely ringed in by these very pigs, and Leroy's up there belting it out as if he's simply speaking in the neighborhood. Panthers don't back down from threats. It's thrilling to listen.

"One of the founding values of the American nation is that citizens have a right to oppose tyranny. To throw off their shackles and demand a government of the people, by the people, and for the people. America can be better! Stand with us. The time to fight has come. All power to the people!"

"Power to the people!" The crowd repeats Leroy's final chant. "Power to the people!"

We hug our stacks of papers, ready to sell, until I see one of the Panthers at the front motioning us even closer. It's someone we know. Guy called Rocco, from the neighborhood.

Rocco takes the papers from me. "Thanks, Maxie-girl.

We were really running low." Rocco's buddy Slim takes some from Emmalee and a guy I don't know takes Patrice's.

"Pretty good sales today, considering," the unknown guy says.

I look at Rocco, confused. "I thought Leroy wanted *us* to help sell them?"

"Nah, we've got it," Rocco says. "Go back to whatever you were doing before."

I don't want to go back. Not to the banner. Not through the crowd. Being close to the guys is better. I can tell by Patrice's expression that she agrees. Emmalee too.

"We're cool," I say, trying to make it sound real casual. "We'll hang here."

Slim nudges Rocco. "Check it, there she is." Kind of under his breath.

In this case, "she" is a sister goes by the name of Cherry. Cherry dresses to kill and there are always casualties. Today it's tight stretchy pants that cup her butt just so. All the brothers turn to look one by one as she passes. Her powder-blue Panther work shirt has been tailored to fit her hourglass shape. A gold belt cinches her waist to almost nothing. A wrist of bangles and a pendant that falls in the line between her breasts. Her jacket dangles from the fingers of one hand. It is warm out, but that's not why she does it. You can tell from the gleam in her eye.

"Hey, everybody."

"Hey, Cherry."

I try not to show that I'm watching her too. Emmalee and Patrice probably, as well. It's no secret between us that we all want to get to look like Cherry in the next five years. Emmalee and Patrice at least have started to grow in the chest. I'm just small all over.

Slim leans forward. "Umm-umm. Cherry, you are looking fine today, girl."

Cherry fixes a gaze on him. She's wearing big shades, but you can tell that's what she's doing. "Today? I always look fine," she quips.

"I hear that." Slim grins back. "I'm just saying."

Cherry slides on by. I watch her go, thinking how nice it would be if I could actually look like that someday.

"I want to go home," Patrice declares a short while later. And it's the second time, and there's more urgency in her voice. "I have a bad feeling. I want to go now." She might be about to cry.

"I want to stay," I tell her. "We have to stay." Bobby hasn't spoken yet. Something more is going to happen. I can feel it. Something I have to be a part of.

But the thing with us is, we always have each other's backs, so something's got to give. We look to Emmalee for the tiebreak. She thinks about it. Emmalee is like that, always thinking things out. You can tell when she's doing it by the look on her face.

"I want to go now, too," she decides. "Sorry, Maxie. We stayed longer than we were going to."

It's not dark yet. All I promised Raheem was that we would leave before dark. But it's two against one.

"Okay. Let's go." We snake through the crowd, moving from Panther to Panther, looking for Hamlin or Raheem to tell them we're off.

"Heem." I see him, finally. "We're going home now."

"You have your tokens?" he says.

I nod. Hamlin had given us two el tokens each, just in case something happened and we needed the extra fare.

"You'll be fine," he says, but I think it's mostly so he won't worry after we go.

"Yup." I'm confident. There's nothing about this crowd we can't handle, even when it's freaking us out. If nothing else, we've proved we're no kind of chickens today.

Raheem points us in the direction he thinks will get us out fastest. We're working our way that way when a big hand catches hold of my shoulder. I hold back a gasp and spin around, ready to scream, ready to fight, ready for anything.

"Maxie?" It's Leroy Jackson. "Can you do me a favor?"

CHAPTER 6

WE BURST FROM THE CROWD ONTO THE sidewalk, heaving deep breaths. "What were you thinking?" Patrice screeches at me. "I'm not going back in there."

"What was I supposed to do?" I feel bad about breaking our deal, but Leroy Jackson's the highest-up Panther I've ever personally met, and he looked me in the eye and said, "Go find some change." Handed me a whole ten-dollar bill. I couldn't say nothing to that but "Yes, sir."

As quickly as we can, we skirt the police barricade and cross the street away from them. Although there's really no getting away. The line of cops looks thicker than ever. It's late afternoon, and I remember what Raheem said about the sun going down.

"I'm going home." Patrice's voice strays to a higher pitch.

"Go home, then," I tell her. "You too." Emmalee raises her eyebrows at me. "I can handle it myself."

"I don't want you going back in there either," Patrice wails. "Did you see how they were looking at us?"

I keep my voice level. "I can do it. It'll probably be faster, even. I'm small. I'll slip right through them like a slice of night. They won't even see me coming." I try to smile.

Patrice is skeptical. She fixes me with a look that says she knows better, and she probably does, but I already told Leroy yes and took the money, so what am I going to do?

"It'll be okay." I do my best to reassure her. "I'll just go home with Hamlin and Raheem."

"Fine," Emmalee says. "I don't want to stand around here any longer." She's right. Too many cops. We stand out like a whole fist of sore thumbs.

Patrice hugs me like she thinks I'm going to die in a minute. I hope she's being overdramatic, but I hug her back because you really never know. I wait until they disappear around the corner, then I make my way along the sidewalk in the other direction. Looking for a store, a Laundromat, whatever I can find.

Leroy's ten-dollar bill is still clutched tight in my fist. Today, more people than normal are paying with dollar bills and expecting change, he said. I smooth it out and try to act like a person who's supposed to have ten whole dollars in her possession.

I luck out. There's a corner store at the end of the block.

fireinthestreets

I duck inside, wait in line behind a bunch of demonstrators buying cigarettes and pop.

When it's my turn the fat white clerk glares at me, gnawing the life out of a toothpick with his jaw. "What do you want?"

"I need a roll of quarters," I say, holding up the bill. He looks at me, at the money, and I can see it settle over his face. Suspicion. It's like he knows by looking that it's not that usual for me to have ten bucks in my hand. I want to be angry, knowing exactly why he thinks that, but I can't quite get there 'cause it's also kind of true.

Clerk looks me up and down. "Ain't got none to spare." Toothpick moves to the other side of his mouth. "Get along out of here." He shoos me with his hand. I flee back to the street, but I try to look calm the second I get out there. Can't go running out of a store with all these cops around. Not smart.

Walking farther, I quickly learn that getting change is a bigger deal than I realized. Two whole blocks and four stores later I'm starting to wonder if I'll ever get a different kind of response. The last guy yelled at me good. "I don't do favors for your kind. Nothing in the law says I have to."

I want to cry, want to give up, but Panthers don't back down from nothing. I go on, my footsteps carrying me where I least wanted to have to go. A real bank building.

There's one right there on the corner, with a nice clean sign out front. It looks exactly like the sort of place I'm not supposed to go. I've never even been inside a bank before, but it is where they keep all the money. I take a deep breath.

The wooden doors are tall and heavy, carved with fancy ruts and swirls. Big, round gold metal handles. I slip inside. It's cool in here. Fans blowing and clean white walls that go high. Big glass lights that hang from the ceiling like bakery birthday cakes upside down. The floor is interesting. There's one big rug that goes all the way to the wall on all sides, but then there are other small rugs on top of it. A square one by a row of chairs, and a long skinny one that leads right up to the counter. I walk along it, feeling like I'm entering a royal palace.

Except I'll never pass for the sort of girl who fits in a place like this. I figure most royalty isn't sweat-dirty with frazzed-out hair and only ten whole dollars.

The woman behind the counter says, "Can I help you?" The sign above her head says TELLER. So I go up and tell her.

"I need a roll of quarters, please." I hold out the ten dollars.

She takes it and holds it up to the light.

"It's real," I blurt, then wish I'd kept my big mouth shut. Saying too much can get you in trouble, Raheem says. Don't I know it. Still, this is advice I'm not good at following.

The teller smiles. "I know. See?" She holds it where I can see. There's a little shadow face next to the big face, in a space that's supposed to be white. "It's called a watermark. All the real bills have them."

"Wow." I'm relieved. Of course, I knew it was real all along, but the bill's already in her hand, and I don't know how I'd get it back if she didn't believe me.

She puts the bill into her drawer and pulls out a roll of quarters. She slides it toward me. "Here you go."

"Thanks." The quarters are wrapped in smooth paper. They're a touch heavier than I would have thought. "This was hard to get," I admit. She seems like a nice person. She helped me.

She smiles again, this time in a way that seems a bit sad. "Well, now you know where to go."

"Thanks," I say again. I pivot on the carpet, start my royal exit. This time, I feel taller. Much more princess-like. Before I push back out into the heat I look back at the teller, wondering what it would be like to go to work in a place where people are rich enough to buy rugs to put on top of the rugs that are already there.

C H A P T E R 7

'VE LOST A LOT OF TIME. THE AFTERNOON LIGHT
is no longer quite as full. I only hope Leroy will know
I did the very best I could. As cut down as I've felt all
day, I'm buoyed by my contact with the woman in the
bank. She was white, and she was nice. I've seen it before,
just not that often. I feel lighter. Right up until the moment
I push back into the throng.

I was right about one thing: I'm so much smaller alone.
At times I think I'll be trampled. I thought I was used to it,
the loudness and the whiteness and the crush of constant
moving feet, but the energy has shifted, and it only keeps getting worse. My breath comes shallower and shallower till I'm
afraid it'll stop altogether. I need a bit of space around me,
need to see what's coming 'fore it smacks me in the face. As it
is, I'm adrift in a sea of blond hair, brown hair, pale skin, fren-
zied eyes. Their frantic energy is the type that wants to con-
sume things—air, time, people—whatever gets in the way.

It's a while before I realize I'm totally lost. I can't see the stage, nor even the speaker poles poking up over anyone's head. Earlier, when I lost sight of it, I relied on Emmalee's height. She could always stretch up and see. Now I don't have anything to go by.

"Please," I call. "I need to get to the stage." I don't think anyone hears.

I'm so close to tears, my face hurts. I can't fail. Not at the first real assignment I've ever been given. And by Leroy himself. I can't let him down.

I try again. "Help. Which way is the stage?"

I'm mad, so mad at myself for screwing this up. I have to show Leroy, show everyone, that I can do it. I can do anything a Panther should do. I walked right into that bank, and everything turned out okay. I try to get that royal feeling back but it's long gone.

It's hopeless. The thought settles over me. I try to push it away, because I know what hopeless feels like, and I don't feel it anymore, not since the Panthers. In this one moment, though, I don't know quite what to hope for. I don't see how I'm ever going to find them again, and it no longer feels like there's much light in the sky. The crowd is furious, it's going to get dark, and I'm supposed to go home.

It all wars out in my mind, but the thought of letting down Leroy hurts me hardest.

"Where is the stage?" I scream. In front of me, someone points. I try to shift, try to go that way, but the momentum of the crowd drives me back. I'm no longer moving upstream; I'm moving backward with the current, and a moment later, the strangest thing I can imagine happens. I'm spun around, see the pale blue flash of uniforms, and am ejected from the crowd amid a mighty swell of screams. I fall to my knees on the sidewalk of a street I don't recognize, at the feet of a row of riot-dressed cops with clubs out and big plastic crowd-pushers in their hands.

I scramble to my feet. *Crowd, not cops. Crowd, not cops*, is all that flashes through my mind. I'd rather be tossed in the crowd forever than face the pigs. Diving desperately, I skid through the edge of the grass on sweaty hands and aching knees. The roll of quarters is sticky in my fist, and I know in that instant I'm never going to make it. I've failed.

Hauling myself to my feet so I don't get trampled, I discover I'm still too close to the edge of things for comfort. The line of cops advances at us like a wall. Behind them, at the corner of the street, two lumbering city buses pull in, nearly mowing down a couple of guys who scramble out of the way at the very last second. The bus doors open and more riot-dressed cops pour out of them into the crowd, a rippling flood of blue helmets streaming forth like water from the tap. Protesters scream as the cops try to drive them back, swinging their batons high and bringing them down hard.

People go running around me, pushing forward. I let them pass, let them get between me and the frightening sights at the clash line. They jostle and push, and I feel like I'm fighting a current. I don't understand, and I don't know where to turn.

It hasn't grown cooler with the dusk. The sun sinks low behind the skyline, stale rays peeking through the avenues in the last gasp of daylight. Someone has a bullhorn. "This demonstration ends at dusk. The park is closing. Please disperse. Please disperse."

Raheem's warning looms large in my mind. *"Promise me you won't stay in the park after dark. Stuff tends to happen when the sun goes down."*

The bullhorn squawks again, but the crowd's chant has changed. A small group near me is calling, *"To do what's right, we'll stay all night. You can't scare us with your might!"*

Skirting the edge of things, I can see how it's all turning bad. The cops are over here, too, lined up and helmeted with clubs out and pushing people back with their big plastic shields. I know enough to stay away from the cops, but everyone else seems to be rushing forward. It's happening around me and I'm fighting the forward surge. You *never* go toward the cops.

Shadows begin to stretch over everything. I'm afraid to stay, but more afraid to leave. I don't want the cops to see me. That's when it hits me. I don't want them to see me, because I'm not allowed to do what everyone around me is doing.

They are angry. Angry on the outside, allowed to let it show. Not like us.

At least, not until the Panthers came along and said we can't wait anymore. Can't be pressed down anymore. It's time. That's what's happening here. People are standing up.

They're protesting for peace, but they're angry. It covers everything, this miraculous, captivating, overwhelming force that's already thrumming in me deep. It swells in great waves, stirring the air like wind beneath a fire. I can feel suddenly how hot it's burning, how the heat of the day didn't start in the sky, but here among us.

I can't leave this place. Not yet. This place where everything is stirred out in the open. Anger, with no fear. Raheem would say it's 'cause they're white; he says you can do anything if you're white, that everything's okay if you're white, but we're not white and never going to be. He doesn't come out and say the rest, but I get it. That nothing is ever going to be okay for us. Except, the Panthers—the Panthers say we gotta try harder and then maybe it can be.

The Panthers say get angry, don't bother to tamp

it down. The Panthers say get busy, trying to make the change happen 'cause it sure ain't happening on its own. I've been going to Panther class long enough to understand what's happening here tonight. The demonstrators are white, they're screaming and bearing down on the police, but nothing more is happening.

I want to do it too, but I can't. *"When the law comes down, it comes down on us."* I have to get out of here. Now.

But, strangely, I find myself sliding back in among them, joining in the chant at the top of my lungs.

CHAPTER 8

THE FEAR RETURNS LIKE A THUNDERBOLT strike. People are running and screaming. The police have entered the park. The sky is dark, and I've been chanting, like a reckless fool, like some wannabe white.

I flee.

The protest has spilled beyond the park. Protesters have taken to the streets. Flashing lights brighten the darkness, and I stay as far as I can from the edge of things. It doesn't stop me from seeing too much. Protesters—white ones—being handcuffed and dragged. Cops with their clubs swinging up and down, and I see it more clearly than ever, why we're supposed to call them pigs.

I have el tokens in my pocket and ten dollars' worth of quarters in my hand, but neither is any use to me, because I'm not going that far out of my way. I edge out of the park as close to the lake side as I can get, sending up a prayer that the pigs won't see and catch me.

It's a long way home, on foot. A matter of hours, it seems. By the time I'm back in the neighborhood, I'm exhausted of running, dodging cruisers, ducking into alleys when they fishtail around corners, screaming toward something that seems to be everywhere. I thought it'd be okay, once I got far enough away, but what is far enough?

Even the neighborhood has caught the reckless spirit of the day. Fires burn ugly in the storefronts. People run in the streets, some looking for safety, others for something else to set aflame. Sirens rage against the night.

Tonight is bad enough on its own, but in the midst of it all my mind is thrown back to the day Dr. King was murdered. The terror and sadness of those nights. To be wrapped in what is awful. No way out, no chance to breathe through the smoke.

I see my building ahead, but I can't even feel relieved yet. So much has happened between this corner of the street and my front door. It's where Bucky was beaten. Where I found Sam throwing rocks into a storefront the night Dr. King died, which was the moment it all sank in for me that everything had changed in the most irretrievable way. It's the sidewalk I've fled down a hundred times, sometimes to get home but most times to get away.

A stretch of road that sometimes brings me to tears. I don't know why I have no tears tonight. My clothes and body are drenched with sweat, so maybe that was all the water in me.

CHAPTER 9

IT'S ALL I CAN DO TO CLIMB THE STAIRS. I OPEN the apartment door and Raheem storms at me like he's been standing there awhile, all wound up and waiting.

"Jesus, Maxie. Where have you been?"

I brush past him, wanting to get indoors. "I'm here now."

"You were supposed to be home!"

"I know." Him being mad is making me mad, and I've had about all I can take for tonight.

"The streets are a goddamn pigsty!" he shouts. "What are you trying to do to me?"

"I got lost," I shout back. "I was trying to get Leroy his quarters." The roll is locked in my fist; it's hard to pry my fingers from their death grip.

"Nobody cares about any damn quarters, Maxie," Raheem yells. "Are you okay?"

"Yes!"

"Okay, then." Raheem throws himself down on the couch. Jumps right back up again. "We don't know what's happening," he blurts. "Daley might order a shoot-to-kill again."

Like after Dr. King? I close my eyes. Not that I have to close them to remember. When the neighborhood was burning for days and days, and no one knew what to do to make it stop because the pain burned hotter than any fire. It still hurts; might as well have been yesterday. Sam and I walked home from school that night, as if everything was usual, and then out of nowhere, people started roiling around us. We made it all the way to my block before we really noticed the commotion, and we didn't know what it was about, so we said good night and went our separate ways. I went into my building and found a cluster of mamas screaming in the stairwell, sick and crying over the news. Dr. King had been shot and killed in Memphis.

The truth slammed down on me like a flat, heavy weight. I couldn't climb any farther after hearing it, so I ran back into the street, as if I could get out from under. Not the smartest thing, Raheem told me later, but at the time I couldn't help it. Sam was out there, and the first thing in my mind was to get back to him.

He hadn't got very far. He was crying, like me, and shaking, like me, and throwing rocks against the broken windows of the shop across the street, which hadn't occurred to me yet but seemed like a good idea. *"Sam,"* I said. He turned around toward me, and I could already start to see emptiness about him, like a mirror of what I felt. We held hands and ran as far and fast as we could, but the weight was on us and there was no escape.

The riots lasted for days. Dr. King was everything for a long while there, and when ".everything" got shot, all that seemed to be left was a whole bunch of nothing. It was no wonder to me why people were raging; you got to fill a space like that with something.

But then the cops rolled through, trying to quell the rage with bullets. The order came straight down from the mayor himself: Shoot to kill any rioters. People died those nights. Shot in the street like stray dogs. Tonight the whole city seems to be on fire. Again.

"Do you hear me?" Raheem says. "They'd be shooting at the white rioters, maybe, but definitely at us. I don't want you out there."

"I'm in," I whisper. I sink onto the couch, feeling smaller than my quietest voice can make me.

Raheem stands over me for a while, looking all mad, but I've said everything I can and the bad part is more or less over. He can't let it go, though, because it's not the kind of night where anything cools down. Finally he walks to the window, stares down into the street. Whatever he sees makes him mutter to himself.

I kick my feet up on the couch. I'm much too grimy to be sitting on the furniture, and I ache to scrub myself clean, but first I need a few moments to just be still. Let my gaze roam anywhere it wants. Study the ceiling, the walls, places where the paint has chipped, the edges of the furniture where the fabric has frayed. The slightly burned corner of the big floor rug. Nothing is perfect, but when it's just the two of us in here alone, the apartment feels like a pocket. All safe and close. Nothing from the outside can get in.

Raheem turns away from the window, no longer mad — at least not at me. He comes and sits on the floor beside the couch, leaning against it.

I let it all rest for a while, thinking. Raheem reaches over and touches my filthy, grass-stained skin. My forearm is scratched and, sure enough, kind of green. I move it out from under his hand. His face holds all these questions and I can't let him ask a single one.

"Did Bobby Seale speak?"

"Yeah." Raheem's eyes glow. "He was great. People got really turned on to what we're doing." He thumps his fist on the cushion. "Before it all went to hell."

"Oh." Flakes of disappointment. I missed it.

Raheem studies my face awhile, but lets the questions

drop. I'm safe now, so maybe he figures it doesn't matter where I've been. Only I know different.

We lie there, staring out the window at gray plumes of smoke rising, at the slight red glow on the sky. He stretches his arm up on the couch near mine again. We don't say it at all, but we're waiting. Waiting for Mama to come home safe from work, which won't be till late. Waiting for the light of day, for it to be okay to go outside again, because that's what we prefer.

The color of the sky is strange and unsettling. Not red enough to speak for itself, just glowing with a reflection of everything roiling below. The whole city is burning, it seems, but I wonder how it manages to bleed onto the sky.

A fire is like that, I guess. Licking from one surface to another, from one person to another, until everything is glowing red and melting.

CHAPTER 10

THE SHOWER MAKES ME FEEL ABOUT 1,000 percent better. I stand beneath the spray for a long, long while, running it cool. Watching the soapy, dirt-tinged water swirl down the drain until it runs clear and I imagine the day has been fully flushed away.

I turn the water off before I'm really ready, but I know there's only so much that can be dealt with on the surface of things. The knot in my stomach is still there. The memory of losing myself among the chanting crowd. The absolute high of the power of that kind of freedom. For the first time ever, I realize what a weight it is to carry fear every time I walk down the street. Always wondering, will the pigs be watching? Will today be the day I can't get away?

I put on my nightgown and come out to the living room. By this point, Raheem is wearing his shorts and undershirt. He's at the window again, looking out. Raheem opens his mouth to say something, but then there's a knock at the door.

"Who is it?" He heads over there.

"Lucille Junkitt." Our neighbor down the hall.

Raheem opens the door. "Hi, Mrs. Junkitt."

She's in her slippers, hair in rollers under a shower cap. "Your mama called. I told her it's not safe trying to get home, so she's staying with someone from her job tonight. Everything okay here?" She pokes her head in to get a look at me. "Maxie?"

"We're fine, Mrs. Junkitt."

She nods. "Y'all let me know if you need anything, you hear?"

We promise to do so, then Raheem locks and bolts the door behind her. He starts back to the window.

I step into his path. "Don't watch. We shouldn't watch anymore."

"You're right," he says, hands on my shoulders. "It's late. Let's just go to sleep."

We go to the room we share. Our beds are parallel, pushed to opposite walls of the room. I slide under my single top sheet. Even though it's warm, I can't fall asleep if I'm exposed.

I reach for my bottom dresser drawer and pull out

Little Ralphie, my stuffed brown dog. He's gotten kind of ratty, and he lives in the drawer most nights, but I still love him. When I get him out, Raheem usually teases me about being too old for toys, but tonight he doesn't comment. He picks up some laundry we've got strewn about the room and tosses it toward the closet.

We put up a curtain some while ago. My half. His half. It's not an even split; I have no window. No privacy either: He comes through my space because I have the door. I can always hear him breathing in his sleep; I'm grateful he doesn't snore.

Tonight Raheem lies straight on top of his covers. He folds his hands beneath his head and stares at the ceiling.

I roll onto my side, facing Raheem, and hug Little Ralphie. Plenty goes without saying around here, and it's nice when we end up on the same page. Like the way he knows tonight is not a night to draw the curtain.

CHAPTER 11

WHEN I WAKE UP, MAMA'S SITTING on the edge of my bed, stroking my hair.

"I didn't mean to wake you."

"Then why are you poking me in the head?" I mumble.

Mama kisses my face. "Why do you insist on following in your brother's footsteps? I don't like you going to all these protests. What are they having you do there?"

A little flurry of panic in my belly. "It's mostly holding signs and stuff. I'm fine, Mama."

Her fingers frame my face. "I didn't say I was going to stop you. I know it's important. I just worry about you."

"Oh."

She sighs. "We have eggs. Do you want me to make you some?"

I sit up. "No, I'm going down to The Breakfast, like I always do."

Mama frowns. "What's this breakfast you're always going to?"

"Mama, I *told* you. It's the Panthers' Free Breakfast. They do it for all the schools in the neighborhood."

"You got another week of summer. Why are you trying to go down to school early?"

I groan. "*Mama.* It's breakfast and it's free."

She shakes her head. "Free food's never really free."

"This one is." I swing my legs out of bed and stand up. "Capital F-R-E-E. Free." This is a word I know exactly how to spell.

"I didn't raise no charity case," Mama says. "You don't gotta give them nothing in exchange for all that food?"

"Well, I volunteer at the office," I say. "That's something."

"Hmm. I still don't like it." Mama gets proud sometimes about wanting to take care of us. Raheem is the same way, but at least he's practical about it. We've had low times around here, times when the Panther Breakfast was the only whole meal I got to eat in a day, and I can't forget that, even if Mama wants to pretend.

"Go away now. I have to get dressed," I tell her.

With a huffy little "Okay, then," she glides out of the room.

CHAPTER 12

GO DOWN TO THE SCHOOLYARD A BIT EARLY.
I want to get there in time for the morning lineup. The
Panthers form ranks on the blacktop and Leroy leads
them in chants.

There they stand in dark straight rows. In the rising
light of morning, taking in the fresh air feels like breathing
new life. I linger outside the fence, watching Leroy up on
his milk crate, presiding over the ranks. Fist raised, he calls
out, "Power to the people!"

The Panther columns answer back, a deep, thunderous
roar like a single massive voice: "Power to the people!"

I close my eyes, pretend I'm standing among them. It
feels good. Shoulder to shoulder with my brothers and sisters in arms. Feels like we can take on the world, one day at
a time. One pig at a time, some days. Build a world where
batons don't crush and white doesn't always equal right.

After being in the crowd last night, I see everything

anew. The Panthers are going to change everything. I've known it all along, but now I can feel it all the way through me.

The convention is still going on downtown. I suppose a crew of Panthers will be going again today, but I know I can't go back. My place is here. In the neighborhood. Not up in a whole white riot. One close call is enough for me.

I lace my fingers through the chain link, wishing I was over there with the rest of them. Fourteen isn't old enough to be a full-on Panther, everyone says. We're supposed to be part of the young Panthers for another couple of years. Go to The Breakfast, go to political education class on Wednesdays and the Freedom School on Saturdays with the little kids, looking smart all lined up with berets cocked this way and that. I help take care of the young ones and tell them what I know, but the real Panthers sometimes look at me like I'm also still a baby who needs to learn. But I know plenty. I've been around the block enough times to know the size and shape of things. I'm ready. I know it.

I look through the fence at the most familiar face in the lineup. Sam is the exception, I guess. Probably because of his brother, Steve, who was one of the first Chicago Panthers. Steve died being a Panther too. Or maybe Sam gets an exception because of his dad, who is Roland

Childs. Mr. Childs is well-known around the neighborhood because he's a civil rights movement leader like Dr. King was. He makes speeches and plans big demonstrations that Raheem used to take me to, before the Panthers came along.

From his perch on the milk crate, Leroy Jackson starts leading the ranks in a series of chants. I've seen it many times before. He starts them out simple, then gets them all riled up.

"Who we gonna be?"

"The Black Panther Party."

"I can't hear you. . . . Who we gonna be?"

"The Black Panther Party." The echo rings loud throughout the schoolyard. It resonates. Deep. People passing by can't help but turn to look.

So much power radiates from the Panther lineup. All this pent-up energy, so huge and so tight that you can practically see it steaming off them. That runaway feeling just come to a standstill, that terrible, terrible anger. Always in control, always just beneath the surface.

In the white newspapers, they use it against us. They make the Panthers look like we all just want to rip the throats out of some white folks for no good reason. We have good reasons, but we still don't want to do that.

"What's it all about?"

"It's all about the people."

Fred and Leroy want to open people's minds, is what Raheem always says. They don't want us to kill; they want us to be willing to die.

We're dying anyway, I can't help but think. Remembering about Steve, and others.

"How we gonna live?" Leroy shouts.

"Gonna live for the people."

"How we gonna die?"

"Gonna die for the people."

"Power to the people!"

"Power to the people!"

"Power to the people!"

Patrice slips up beside me, laces her fingers through the chain link, too. "Hey, Maxie."

To be honest, I'm not that happy to see her. I don't want to do this now. There's a part of me that wishes we were in an actual fight, so I could get away without speaking to her for a day or so.

"Hey."

"So I guess everything went all right?"

Reluctantly I show her the roll of quarters, which I have in my pocket. In the daylight it looks all mangled and sweaty.

"Oh, no. What happened?"

Not answering seems safest.

Patrice throws her arm around my shoulders. "It's going to be fine," she says. "I'm sure it's not a big deal."

It's a very big deal. To me. I've never worried before about not having what it takes to be a Panther. If I can't carry through even the smallest task, am I also going to crumble when something real falls to me?

CHAPTER 13

THE BREAKFAST TABLES ARE ALL LINED UP in the schoolyard, as long as the weather's good. Sam's serving up sausage and gravy, so there's no avoiding him this morning.

"Hey, Maxie," he says.

"Hey." I stand there, holding the plate he handed me, until Emmalee nudges me to move along down the line. One of the mamas comes bustling over with a fresh pan of gravy from the kitchen. Piled atop it, a tray of hot biscuits steaming into the muggy August air.

She clucks her tongue at us. "Don't you get out of this line 'fore you have some apple slices on those plates," she says. "You need fruit."

We stand obediently until a second mama comes hurrying up to replenish the fruit bowl. She spoons apple slices onto our plates, while another woman comes up behind her with jugs of orange juice. I wonder exactly how many mamas are back there cooking. My stomach rumbles as I take the cup that she pours for me and follow Patrice toward one of the long tables to sit.

With the edge of her plate in my back, Emmalee steers me to the side of the table where I'll be facing away from Mr. Sam Childs. It's been their mission all summer to get me to leave him alone. Ever since things went bad, which is basically since Steve died, I've been fighting it, but the girls say it's time to give it up.

"You better not get gravy on me," I threaten.

"Too late," she squeaks.

I convulse myself trying to look back there. Patrice busts out laughing. Emmalee too. "I'm just messing," she admits.

We dig into the food. I can't help thinking how it always used to be Steve who served at The Breakfast, along with Raheem and some other guys, in shifts. I miss Steve. We all do. His big personality and his smile that could light up the room. The Breakfast was most fun on the days when he and Raheem would get up front together and crack jokes on each other till we were all about to choke for laughing. Steve was best friends with Raheem, so it was all in good fun. I knew him longer than Sam, really, because he was over sometimes. Even slept on our bedroom floor a few nights once, when things were rough for him at home.

There's a hole in things now. Sam is different. Raheem is different. Everything's changed.

I look over my shoulder. Some days I resist it, but today isn't one of them. I miss Steve, sure, and that's a forever thing. Not reversible. Nothing I can do. But I miss Sam, too.

C H A P T E R **1 4**

'M SO EXCITED TO SEE THE NEW PANTHER OFFICE. We go straight there after breakfast.

"Ooh, look," Emmalee says, sounding as enthralled as I feel. They've taken the brown paper out of the windows. The clean, clear glass is printed with the words THE BLACK PANTHER PARTY in one window and the large black cat logo in the other. The glass door to the right of the windows bears a smaller version of both. Right now it's propped open with a stacked pair of bricks, and the moment we step inside the reason for that is clear.

It smells a lot like fresh paint in here, but other than that it looks great. It's nice and bright, with the big front windows, at least compared to the old second-floor apartment where the Panthers used to be based. The front room alone is bigger than the old Panther apartment, too, maybe by half. It doesn't look as lived-in yet, without the bulletin boards on the walls with clippings and posters and things. The only thing hanging so far is a large size poster-portrait of Huey Newton. Everyone loves this picture of him, where he's sitting in an arch-backed wicker chair with a rifle in one hand, a traditional African spear in the other, and this look on his face that says "Don't mess with me." It's become something of a banner for the party, Huey being one of the founders and all.

There are three big desks in the room, arranged in a loose U shape. A row of battered metal file cabinets line the back wall, right up to the door that leads to another room in the back. There's a couch against one wall, near several rickety bookcases chock-full of titles from the Panthers' recommended reading list. A lending library for members. Emmalee goes straight to it.

I think some of the furniture is the exact same, moved down from the old apartment. It just looks smaller with all the space around it. And more used, with the fresh light pouring in on it.

Rocco's sitting on the edge of the front desk, reading the daily newspapers. He's got them all spread out next to him like he's trying to gift wrap the desktop. "Hey, Maxie-girl. You okay? We were afraid you got caught in the thick of it."

"Oh, I'm okay," I say quickly. "Where's Leroy?"

"I'm here." He emerges through the doorway of the rear room. "Maxie, I'm glad you're all right."

"Yes, fine." My fingers are trembling as I hold out the mangled roll of quarters. "Here's your ten dollars."

"Okay." He takes the roll. Doesn't comment on its condition as he takes a seat at the desk.

"I'm sorry," I blurt. "I did my best to get back to you, but the crowd . . ." My voice trails off. The telephone rings from across the room, filling my silence.

"I feel bad I even asked you," Leroy says. "Didn't think it through."

"I wanted to help," I declare, needing him to know I can handle another assignment. "I tried, but I couldn't get back to the stage. Everyone was pushing me."

Leroy frowns. "Did anyone hurt you? Or the other girls?"

"We're fine." I try to pull myself tall. Don't want to sound like I'm making excuses. "You don't have to worry."

"Leroy, phone," Hamlin calls.

Leroy slides out of his chair. "It's my job to worry, Maxie," he says, tapping my shoulder with his fist as he passes.

CHAPTER 15

THE NEWSPAPER HEADLINES TELL THE story of last night in clear, sharp pictures. Rocco spreads them out so I can see, too. It screams from the pages of the *Chicago Sun-Times*, the *Chicago Tribune*, and even the *New York Times*: ANTI-WAR GROUPS CLASH WITH POLICE.

Patrice leans over my shoulder, looking also. I read the headlines, but I'm not going to bother to struggle through the articles themselves. If it matters for us at all, Patrice will tell me what it said later. She knows I can't read well, even though I try hard. Patrice has always been good at helping me. Emmalee didn't used to help because she said if she did, I would never learn. Sometimes she still can't understand how I can practice reading all the time and not get any better, but now she has this theory that there's probably something up with my brain. Good at talking, bad at reading. That's me. So I skip the words, but the pictures I study carefully. I wonder for a second what it would be like to be a photographer in a crowd like that. Standing still while everything happens, trying to capture it. It feels like I have a camera in my mind, somewhat. Snapshots keep coming back to me. Floating to the surface. I'd just as soon forget.

I hear a little gurgling sound, and I turn. Leroy's wife, Jolene, emerges from the back room, her two tiny daughters in tow. Releasing her mama's hand, Nia trots across the room and hugs Patrice's leg. Patrice picks her up and snuggles her, cooing silly words until the little girl giggles. Jolene carries the gurgling baby, Betty, in her arms.

"Oh, good. You're here," she says, sounding relieved. "Will you take her?"

Obediently I cross the room and lift Little Betty out of Jolene's arms. The baby squalls for a second, flailing her chubby fists against me.

"The toys are in the back," Jolene says. "I could really use your help today." Nodding, Patrice scoots by me with Nia, disappearing into the back room.

"Sure," Emmalee says, coming up and teasing Little Betty's plump cheek with a finger. I hold the baby carefully, all the while thinking, I don't want to babysit. I want to be a Panther.

"Thanks, girls." Jolene squeezes my shoulder before

moving to one of the desks. She's off to do important Panther work, I'm sure. If they'd let me, I could help.

Help more, I mean. I pat Betty's soft diapered bottom, trying to reassure myself that babies are important too. They just don't *do* anything.

Leroy hangs up the phone and sighs. "Trouble. Chicago PD is sniffing around Bobby to determine the Panthers' involvement in the rioting last night."

"We weren't involved at all," Hamlin says.

"Try telling that to Mayor Daley and whatever puppet detectives he puts on the case," Rocco interjects.

"Mark my words," Leroy says. "If they can pin this mess on us, they definitely will."

CHAPTER 16

WHEN THE LITTLE GIRLS ARE there, we oftentimes end up watching them so Jolene can get her work done. Patrice and Emmalee prefer playing with Nia, but I like Little Betty because I don't have to do much but hold her. As long as she's quiet and doesn't need to be changed, I can leave the back room and sit on the couches, listening to whatever's going on among the adults.

Other days, we get assigned different small tasks around the office. We clean a lot. We make sandwiches a lot. We have gotten very good at stamping and sealing envelopes. We use a damp sponge so our tongues don't get all dried out and paper-cut.

Letters go out to lots of different people. Leroy writes to ask people for contributions to support the Panthers' community programs, like The Breakfast and the new neighborhood free health clinic. Then he sends them thank-you notes if they send money so that hopefully they'll send more. He writes to other Panther offices around the country, because long-distance phone calling can get expensive. Jolene and Hamlin write a lot of letters to the editors of the white newspapers, but they don't get printed very often.

Sometimes the girls and I go around putting up flyers in the neighborhood, inviting people to join the Panthers or come to political education classes. We copy the flyers on lithograph machines down at the big office-supply warehouse at the edge of the neighborhood. The day clerk secretly lets us use the machines for free. We do it fast in small batches when his boss is out to lunch. We don't have a litho in the office yet.

Today Lester Smith comes trucking in with a giant box and lays it on the desk in front of me, where I've been lurking since Jolene took Little Betty from my arms. "You busy, Maxie?" he says.

I had just been wondering what my next task was going to be. Emmalee and Patrice are still in the back.

"No. What's up, Lester?" He's a beefy guy, like Rocco, but also very friendly. Lester was one of the original neighborhood protection crews, along with Leroy, Raheem, and Steve. The Panthers call what they do "policing the police" because the crews go out with their weapons on and tail the police officers who patrol our neighborhood. If the police get into anything, like harassing people or trying to arrest someone who doesn't deserve it, the Panther crews go over to the scene and just watch the whole thing happen. That way there are witnesses, and sometimes that scares the cops into doing their jobs right and not bothering people.

"Can you sort these?" Lester says.

I peer into the box. It's a jumble of different Panther buttons. It looks like there are a few rolled-up posters underneath. This will be another mindless, silly task, like the ones they always give me. Sometimes I walk the streets pretending I am more important to the Panthers, like a policer is, but mostly I like to avoid the cops, and I don't have a gun or anything, so I always end up back in the office waiting to be assigned something menial.

"It's a mess," Lester says. "Oakland sent us this stuff to sell, but it doesn't all go at the same price, so we ought to keep a handle on how many we have of each."

"Okay," I say quickly. Even though I get grumbly about it on the inside, I know that it's best to be agreeable. I'll do whatever they ask because I want to show I can be a good soldier. Follow orders. Do my part. Every little thing helps, like Leroy's always saying in the meetings.

I remember the first time I heard him say it, how proud it made me feel.

"I hear people all the time saying 'I don't have anything to give.' Everyone's got something. You got a penny to give, we need it. You got a sheet of paper and a stamp, we'll use it. That's money saved. You got an hour to give, give it. Twenty-four people give an hour and that's a whole day's work done. You dig?"

Leroy knows how to make people with nothing feel like something. That's why people come around. The whole time we're in the office, people come in and out. Buying the paper, leaving off books and picking up new ones, poking their heads in and asking about what it is that the Panthers do. So much so that the Panthers have started having someone serve a shift as kind of a receptionist. Someone or a couple of people who sit around jawing about the Panthers' ideas with anyone who happens by. Not real formal at a desk or anything, but over on the couches, like they're just hanging out. The best political education happens on the sly, Leroy says.

Lester fetches me some smaller boxes to sort into. I dig my hands into the big box, hoping not to stick myself. The buttons show lots of different things. THE BLACK PANTHER PARTY. The sprawling panther logo. A silhouette of Huey Newton's head. A black fist. I pick one that says ALL POWER TO THE PEOPLE and pin it to my shirt while I'm working. I'll have to put it back — I can't afford it — but at least I can look the part for a minute.

CHAPTER 17

RUMOR HAS IT, THE DNC DEMONSTRATION today is headed in the same direction as it was yesterday. Cops all lined up and foaming at the mouth to get a piece of the crowd, and the crowd raging right back at them, taunting them. The Panthers are pulling out. We know better than those white kids that you want to be calm when you're getting in the face of the cops. Our policers do it every day. The right way. We don't need to get mixed up in any kind of melee, not like yesterday.

I keep my head down, keep focused on the buttons, while Lester and Leroy talk about it with Gumbo, who just walked in with a report from downtown.

"That's it," Lester says. "White allies are just going to mess with us. I knew it all along."

"We have plenty of white allies," Leroy corrects. "But maybe the anti-war crowd just needs to do its own thing.

They can't see anything but how the world looks to them right now."

"They're never going to see our side," Gumbo agrees. "The street side, I mean. They're all rich kids."

On that note, the office falls into a moment of silence. Panther silence isn't like total silence, though, because you can practically hear the hum of everyone thinking about things.

Into that almost silent hum walks Bucky Willis. All at once, everyone in the office cheers. Bucky has that way about him, lifting the spirits of a room.

I leap up and hug him. Others rush forward to pat him on the shoulders.

"I should come down more often, if I'm gonna get received like that," Bucky jokes. "Heya, Maxie." He keeps his arm around my shoulders.

I duck my face against his chest. "Hey."

Bucky is great, and I know I hold a special place in his heart, but seeing him is kind of a mixed bag because it reminds me of everything he's been through.

"You're welcome anytime, man," Lester says.

Bucky's not a Panther, but he's our best success story here in Chicago, so he's something of a mascot for the office.

I know the story all too well. It was one of those afternoons that starts out normal and ends up being anything

but. Sam walked me home—that was the normal part—
and when we got to my street, we saw Bucky. He was running late for work, literally running down the block, and
when he came around the corner he happened to bump
into two cops coming the other way. It was an accident,
but the cops blamed Bucky, the way that cops do. He tried
to talk his way out, but they got mad and started beating
him with their batons. When I close my eyes sometimes,
out of nowhere, I can still see his bleeding, bruised-up
face. The way he fell limp to the sidewalk, and the way
the cops cursed overhead while they kicked him into the
street.

Afterward, they charged him with assaulting a police
officer and resisting arrest. They put Bucky in jail and held
a big trial, and in the end it was Sam's and my word against
the cops'. We went to court to testify, and it was the scariest
thing I could imagine.

The courtroom was very big and very gray and it was
full of angry glaring white people. A whole row of cops in
uniforms in the front row of chairs, looking mad like they
might leap right over that railing and destroy me. Two
lines of white faces in the jury box, too, and those were the
people I had to look at while I was talking, the judge said.
He sat up tall in the highest seat in the room, looking all-
powerful, robed in black. The lawyers asked me questions

and I told the whole truth, then after I was done I sat out in the hallway and cried. I thought Bucky was going to die in that room for sure. It felt like I'd only escaped by the skin of my teeth, and I wasn't even the one on trial.

Bucky could have gone to jail for a long time, but based on our testimony, the Panthers' legal aid lawyers got him off. It was a miracle.

So when Bucky squeezes my shoulder, I hug him back, and we don't have to say any more about it. We don't need any words, because for that long hour in the witness stand, the only lifeline I had was my frequent glances into his blank, helpless face, and he was always looking right back. There's no way of erasing a connection like that.

When I get upset about not being a real Panther, Emmalee likes to remind me about the time I testified. When Raheem asked me to do it, I thought finally I was doing something that mattered. It did matter, I guess, because I showed them I was brave, but Sam's the one whose testimony actually made a difference. He's the one who people had heard of, because of his famous father. He's the one they believed.

In the midst of the Bucky reception, Patrice sidles up to me. "Can we go now?"

"Okay," I say. She helps me finish sorting the buttons, then we grab Emmalee and skedaddle.

We never spend all day there, especially now that summer is winding down. After we do our part for the day we escape. For Emmalee and Patrice, it's escaping the office work. For me, it's escaping the feeling that I'll never get to do anything important.

CHAPTER 18

THE HEAT OF THE STREETS ON A LATE-summer afternoon. We walk slow, trying not to work ourselves up to dripping. We stare at the sidewalk, step by step, looking for lost coins among the sidewalk cracks, in the gutter. We scope the bus stops especially hard, 'cause we know what happens when people get in a hurry.

"Another dime," Emmalee says, leaning down to scoop it up. Her long fingernails pinch it like a claw.

"How much is that?"

Emmalee shakes her little cloth pouch. Peers into it. "One twenty."

"Damn," says Patrice. "This is taking all day. We shoulda gone downtown."

"Nah, too much hassle," I say. "We're not trying to make rent." All we wanted was enough for a couple of ice cream cones. A buck fifty'd pull us each a cone at Charlie's. The afternoon soda jerk, Jimmy, is sweet on Emmalee.

It takes another half hour before we find enough. My neck is sweat slick under my hair. If my mouth wasn't so dry it'd be watering over the very idea of ice cream.

We pour the coins into Emmalee's hand and double-check the count. One fifty-five. We track back toward Charlie's.

The fan's whirring pretty good inside. Its breeze feels fresh and cool.

Behind the counter, Jimmy nods when he sees us. "Hi, Maxie. Patrice." He smiles. "Hi, Emmalee."

Emmalee's light skin purples. "Hi, Jimmy."

He rubs his hands on his white uniform apron. "What can I get for you ladies? Ice cream?"

Emmalee spills the coins onto the counter. "Three single scoops, please," she says. She smiles and there's this pause while he stares at her like a little puppy.

Patrice and I hang back, let her do her thing. So far, so good. Sometimes she's too shy and we have to swoop in and help out.

"Sure, sure," Jimmy says after a minute, fumbling for the scooper. "What flavor?"

"Mint," I call.

"Vanilla," says Patrice.

"Strawberry. Can you put mine in a sugar cone?" Emmalee says.

Patrice nudges me, but I'm already grinning. Really, really good.

Jimmy takes a sugar cone and leans into the freezer. "A sweet cone for a sweet girl" is what I think he says, though I'm not sure he meant us to hear it.

I bite my tongue, elbow Patrice.

Jimmy scoops the strawberry first. He gives her a big double scoop, despite the fact that we only paid for singles. Like usual.

"You look pretty today, Emmalee."

"Really?" she says. Her fingers touch the edges of the freezer glass.

"Yeah. Real pretty."

"Thanks, Jimmy." She reaches out for the cone. It's a slow exchange, fingers brush. Her cheeks are flushed. You can't tell on him, but I'm betting it's the same.

He lets go, finally, and scoops the mint and the vanilla into regular cones for us. Double scoops. Not as big, but we don't begrudge.

We hop forward to grab them. "Thanks." Fast grab, quick retreat. Handful of napkins and we are out the door.

"Bye, Jimmy." I use my sweetest, drippiest voice.

"Yeah, bye, Jimmy," Patrice echoes in kind. It appears he barely hears us. Half laughing, we retreat to the street, perching on the bench against the window, while Emmalee lingers by the counter, licking her cone.

CHAPTER 19

LET'S GO BACK TO THE OFFICE," I SAY, once Emmalee finally leaves Jimmy to his job and we've wiped our fingers clean.

"I don't wanna work," says Patrice.

"It's important," I tell her.

"I know," she says, "but we never get to do anything fun anymore."

"We just had ice cream."

Patrice rolls her eyes. "But we spent two hours *working* in order to get it."

"School's starting so soon," I say. "We're not going to be able to go there as much."

"Yeah, we'll just be all cooped up indoors someplace else."

"Not the same."

"Yeah-huh. Plus we have PE class tonight. What, do you want us to be all Panthers, all the time?" Patrice knows perfectly well that's what I want.

Emmalee butts in. "Okay, let's go to the park, but while we're there I'll quiz you on the platform. Good enough?"

Patrice shrugs. I put my hands on my hips. "Fine."

We accept Emmalee's compromise by spending the afternoon in the park, working on memorizing the Black Panther Party's Ten-Point Platform and Program. When we become full members, we have to be able to recite it at will, so we figure we should get a jump on it.

"What we want. What we believe," Emmalee prompts. "Number one?"

"'We want freedom,'" I quote. "'We want power to determine the destiny of our Black Community.'"

"'We believe that black people will not be free until we are able to determine our destiny,'" Patrice says.

"Good. Number two?"

"'We want full employment for our people.'" I like this point especially, because it means Mama would always have a job. The second half is trickier, but I take a deep breath and do my best to say it. "'We believe that the federal government is responsible and obligated to give every man employment or a guaranteed income. We believe that if the white American businessman will not give full employment, then the means of production should be taken from the businessmen and placed in the community so that the people of the community can organize and employ all of its people and give a high standard of living.'"

"You got it, word for word," Emmalee says, sounding impressed.

I smile. We already talked about this one, what it means. I remember, because I want it most. A "high standard of living" means always having food and shelter and a warm coat in the winter. The whole paragraph together means that instead of having a bunch of rich white bosses who hire and fire people and make all the money, big businesses should be owned by the people and everyone should share the profits. Raheem says this would be hard to make work in America, but the Panthers want us to try anyway.

"Number three?" Emmalee says.

Patrice pipes in. "'We want an end to the robbery by the white man of our Black Community.' But I forget the second half. . . ."

"It's long," Emmalee says. "It says America owes black people money because of slavery. Let's do number four." She already has the platform memorized, 'cause things like that come easy to her.

"'We want decent housing, fit for shelter of human beings.'" That means good apartment buildings like the one Patrice lives in, or a real house like Sam's. Not like the stinking projects where we live.

"Number five?"

Patrice and I glance at each other. "Um . . ."

"'We want education that teaches us our true history and our role in the present-day society.'" We all know this is Emmalee's favorite. Anything to do with books.

"Right. Number six is: 'We want all black men to be exempt from military service,'" I recall. It's easy to remember the ones that would change things the most for me.

It makes me shiver when I think about the brothers from the block who went to Vietnam. Some of them come back looking like they got ghosts in their eyes. The rest come back in boxes. We have older guys on the block who were in the black regiments in the world war, right on the front lines of everything. One guy in our building is missing a leg, got it blown off in Omaha, which sounds like it might be in Nebraska but is actually a beach in France. I don't want Raheem to be like that.

Plus, it's like Raheem says, we're fighting a war right here, too. For every foreign war wound I can think of around the neighborhood, there's at least one guy got beat down or shot up by a cop or jailed for doing nothing. "'We believe that black people should not be forced to fight in the military service to defend a racist government that does not protect us,'" I whisper.

"Number seven: 'We want an immediate end to police brutality and murder of black people,'" Patrice says.

I go straight into, "Number eight: 'We want freedom for all black men held in federal, state, county, and city prisons and jails.'"

"I don't know," Patrice jokes. "Some brothers need to be locked up." We laugh, but it's only kind of funny, because the ones who go to jail aren't always the ones who deserve it.

"But . . ." Emmalee nudges us, through her smile.

"'We believe that all black people should be released from the many jails and prisons because they have not received a fair and impartial trial.'"

I think about Bucky again, remembering how I took one look at that all-white jury and felt so sure Bucky was a goner, no matter how I testified. We fought for him 'cause it was right, but no one really thought he'd get off. How wrong is that? For the system to be so messed up that we were all sure Bucky was going down even when we knew he didn't deserve it.

"Almost there," Emmalee says. "Finish it out, girls."

"Number nine," Patrice recites. "'We want all black people when brought to trial to be tried in court by a jury of their peer group or people from their black communities, as defined by the Constitution of the United States.'"

It's true. If Bucky had had an all-black jury, I wouldn't have worried about a thing. Because they would know how it is. White folks, even the nice ones, don't always want to believe how bad it really gets for us.

This is why I believe in the Panthers, from my blood and from my soul. Because they know how I feel and they say it out loud.

"Number ten: 'We want land, bread, housing, education, clothing, justice, and peace.'" I put my fist in the air, the Panther salute.

CHAPTER 20

POLITICAL EDUCATION CLASS IS CROWDED this week. I'm sure Leroy, up at the front, is happy about that. The room is hot as a boiler, so it's surprising that people are staying.

After the stifling air, and the crowd, the first thing that gets my attention is Sam. Of course he's here, he's always here. He raises a hand to wave at me. I wave back. Patrice grabs my elbow. "Oh, no, no, no," she says. "Don't start."

"Don't make us read you the list," Emmalee whispers.

"Read it to me," I say, because I see empty chairs near where Sam is sitting.

"You have to give him time to be sad," Patrice says. But it's been four months.

"When you were seeing him every day, you always came home crying," Emmalee says. That's because I was sad, too, over Steve. I still am.

"When you got too close he just got mad," Patrice adds.

It's true. There were some very bad days between us. Days when he yelled at me or ran away. He was no kind of boyfriend for a while there.

"There are lots of better boys out there." That one is just not true. I have a feeling it will never be true.

But I let the girls win me over with the list. We sit at the opposite side of the room from Sam, an unfortunate by-product of which is I can still see him. Sitting there folded into his jacket, despite the heat, with his head bowed, listening.

Leroy takes the stage, which really just means he stands at the front of the community room, but this presence comes over him right when he's about to speak that makes wherever he's standing seem like a stage.

First he talks about membership, for anyone who's new. "The rules for membership are posted in the back," he begins.

I've read the rules. It took me a long time, because there are twenty-six of them. Things like: Panthers cannot drink on duty, or while armed. People who use drugs will be expelled from the party. Panthers cannot harm or take anything from members of the community. Panthers must participate in political education classes. Panthers must never resist arrest, but must know their rights under the law so the police can't take advantage.

"When you join, you will be trained to load, handle, and fire weapons," Leroy says. "This is a serious responsibility of membership—to defend your home and family, as well as the community, against assault from the police. It's an executive mandate from our minister of defense, Huey, remember."

The crowd is listening, but rumbles go up at different points throughout his speech. At the mention of Huey there is a bit of a swell. I find my glance cutting over to Sam, again and again.

"You will swear an oath of commitment to the party and to the people. This means promising to live a life of service and sacrifice, pushing past personal considerations for the benefit of all. Whether you die tomorrow or a hundred years from now, this is a lifelong oath." Leroy pauses, letting the weight of that pronouncement settle over the room. I've heard him say it before, and you can tell by the completeness of the silence that follows that everyone is thinking hard about what it all means.

"Also, the neighborhood free health clinic is now up and running," Leroy announces. People clap and cheer. "Get your checkups there. Get your kids tested for sickle-cell. Get your medicine there. If you're sick, go there.

"Everything's free, but if and when you can chip in, do that so we can keep it going, you dig?"

Murmurs throughout the crowd.

"All right, let's get started with the class. Tonight we'll talk about freeing our minds from the way white people have trained us to think since slavery. We'll talk about different ways of seeing the world, and how we as a community can start to change the way we are viewed as Americans, as black citizens, as Panthers. . . ."

I'm supposed to be listening, but what I'm thinking about is Sam. And the girls' list. And how all the points on it seem to grow less and less important every day.

CHAPTER 21

FTER ALL THE PANTHER CLASSES AND work this summer, regular school seems doubly boring. I'm not loving how I have to fill my head with this white man's history. Now I know the truth. Makes it hard not to shout out in class, hard to keep my fist out of the sky, with them talking about how Christopher Columbus "discovered" America and how all the blacks were written into the laws as two-thirds of a person. Well, they've stuck to that story but good.

I'd rather drop out and be a full-time Panther, but Jolene says I got to keep on. Get good grades and a diploma, go to college, land a good-paying job so I can take care of myself and never have to worry about nothing. "And donate to the Panthers," I say, and she laughs. "Right on."

Plus, she says learning the wrong makes you know right better when you see it. I don't know about that. I think I already know the wrong; something new is what I'm craving.

Sam waits for me on the steps outside of school. He doesn't say anything, so I guess I could just keep going and act like I didn't see. But I know it's me he's waiting for. That's how it always used to go with us. And my heart still flips when he looks at me, no matter how hard I try to hold it steady.

"Can I walk you home?" he says.

In spite of everything, I smile. This is how it used to go. This is how it started. "I know my way home," I say, but quiet. Nicer. Not like I used to, back before I knew he wasn't just any old guy.

I expect him to say something back, like a joke. But everything's changed since then. He just looks up at me with these sad eyes. Says nothing except what's already written on his face. And I'm not sure how to read it.

"Why?" I say. "I really don't want to start over."

"Okay," he says. "Please?"

It's those sad eyes that break me. It didn't used to be a hard thing, walking with him, being with him. What we had came pretty easy, once upon a time. I made him work for it, sure, but underneath the game, we fit real easy.

"I guess." I wave across the yard to Patrice and Emmalee, point at Sam. Putting their heads together, they scamper on without me, leaving us to whatever's about to happen. Then Emmalee turns back, jumping up and down

fireinthestreets

95

to get my attention. She brings the fingers of one hand, then the other, to her lips, blows me a stream of melodramatic kisses. Beside her, Patrice shakes her finger at me.

I roll my eyes—even though they're too far away to see—and flick my hand. I know without question that the two of them are rushing home to lurk by our building, hiding at the corner till he leaves. Waiting for my report.

They annoy me sometimes, but I'm lucky to have them. Mostly, Sam's all by himself. Especially now. I think back, and in the whole time I've known him, he's either been hanging by himself, or with Steve, or with me, or with his family. People like him, but he doesn't really have a tight bunch of friends. Not ones that go way back. Like Steve did. Like I do. Sam has Bucky, and Leroy and the Panthers now, but it's not the same thing.

"Okay, come on," I say, turning toward the gate.

We walk without speaking, and even though it might look like nothing's happening, it isn't how it looks. This is all there is now. Sam's quiet sadness. My uncertainty of what to say or do. We walk, this long, slow, quiet march, and I feel in the air between us that this is as real as it gets.

It's different, other times. He talks, he even laughs. When it's not just us, when we're around people and he puts on his act for the world like everything's okay.

Like now, when we come around the corner onto Bryant

and we pass Rocco and Slim getting out of Slim's car in front of the corner store.

"Sam, my man," Rocco calls, bounding toward us.

Sam lifts his chin. "Hey, Rocco. What's happening?"

They slap hands and have this guy moment going back and forth, talking about who last had the keys to the storeroom at the health clinic.

"Wasn't me," Sam says. "Coulda been Bill or Pinky."

Rocco shakes his head. "It better not be Pinky. That brother can't keep a key to his own damn house in his hand."

"I hear that." Sam laughs.

I stand back and watch them, this thought forming in my mind like a tiny bloom. A thought about how Sam is becoming less Sam and more somebody else. I try to pluck it, pluck it like a weed, but it just keeps growing, digging deeper.

"It'll turn up," Sam says. "I'm keeping an eye out."

"Sure, sure." Rocco waves and sweeps off the way we just came from.

"You're working down at the clinic?" I say, just to keep the talking going. I already heard something about it. Anyway, since the clinic was Steve's pet project and all, it figures that Sam would want to pick it up and keep it going.

"Yeah."

"How do you like it?"

"I like it okay."

We fall back into silence. My mind, a tangle of weeds. Step after step, the part of me that wants to reach out and take his hand fights with the part of me that wants to run away, close my eyes, and try to forget I ever knew him.

When I can see my building up ahead, it's nothing but a relief.

I don't know what Sam sees when he looks in the mirror, but as the days pass I see more and more of Steve, in his face and in his manner. It's the kind of thing that makes me want to hold my breath till it passes, 'cept it doesn't. And I have to let go.

CHAPTER 22

AM KISSES MY CHEEK TO SAY GOOD-BYE. No words. He leaves me outside my building as used to be usual, and sure enough the girls come scampering out of hiding the moment he's out of sight.

"Ooh, you let him kiss you!" Patrice scolds, laughing.

"Are you taking him back?" Emmalee asks.

Is it really that simple? It wasn't like he dumped me. It ended because it had to, because we're not the same as we used to be. Either of us. I touch my cheek, where his lips brushed. "I don't know."

Sam turns my world over in his hands every time he looks at me. Today, especially, I'm spinning. Dizzy to the point where there is ringing in my ears.

Patrice says it's a "crush" and I have to get out from under it. But she's never had a "crush," at least not one who crushed back or held her hand or kissed her, so how would she know? It's a good enough word, I guess. "Crush." It lays me flat sometimes. The whole weight pressing on me. The weight of Sam and his sad eyes. The weight of Steve and his memory, which grows smaller and more blurred every day, but not any lighter to carry.

It feels like a dream sometimes, how it used to be between us. At times like that it's easy enough to believe there's no such thing as love, like Mama says. What I thought we had was never real, this long, slow, happy moment when everything was good. But then I see him, and I know, sure as my palm aches without his up against it. I see him and the breath slips out of my body. It all really happened.

When I can breathe again, I want to curse the sky for tearing us apart. I want to forget his name, his scent, the way his arm twists when he reaches for my hand.

I want to go back to being the girl I was before him.

CHAPTER 23

THE GIRLS AND I SIT IN THE PARK, ON THE brick wall that runs by the basketball courts. It's just a half wall with no kind of function but to separate the grass from the pavement, so you have to walk around it to enter the courts. We've never been sure what it's even doing here, but it makes a nice place to sit and watch stuff happen.

We read aloud to each other, chapters from *The Wretched of the Earth*. The edges of the book curl from being touched by many hands. Emmalee reads soft and clear, but even her gentle voice can't soften the words themselves. She reads about the struggle, the way the people who Have try to fix it so that the rest of us will always Have Not. I think of Mama, trying to keep a job, and that edge of fury about Raheem as he counts his pay like it's never going to be enough, no matter what; never going to be enough hours in the day to make ends meet.

The words are stirring, the sun is baking, and I feel my skin begin to burn, inside and out.

Emmalee hands the book to me. I don't especially like it when it's my turn to read. Emmalee does better. But she practices more, not just for homework but also for fun. Books from the library, all stacked by her bed. Patrice too. Her family has books on the wall, all up in a whole big bookcase. Fat books and thin books, fact books and storybooks, all jumbled together—a whole store of tiny printed words. Not like me. Holding the book's paper spine is a little bit foreign to me. It's not like the thick shell of our school books, heavy as knowledge and hard to crack through. It's easy to turn these pages. But my tongue trips over the sound of things like they can never become a part of me, even when I want them to be, even when they already are. Emmalee helps me sound words out. We look them up in her pocket dictionary; there are a lot I don't know. It makes it seem true, what Raheem says about needing to stay in school, if there's ever going to be a chance for something better for any of us. He thinks I can get a good job in an office, the kind Mama dreams of but isn't smart enough for, she sometimes says. But I am, they say. Smart enough. Raheem thinks if I learn more words, and how to type them, I'll be okay.

Once when he was mad at me for not shutting up, he

keklamagoon

said I might as well be a lawyer in a courtroom, 'cause I can talk people's ears off. I liked that idea especially, and for a while I pictured myself like a businesswoman on TV, wearing a skirt suit and my hair up all pretty, with a briefcase and a head full of important things to say like "cross-examine" and "My client pleads not guilty." It was fun for a little while, but afterward I got mad right back at Raheem for even bringing it up. I don't know why he put an idea like that in my mind. We both know it can't happen. There's a whole lot of school between me and the courtroom, unless I get real far into the Panthers, and then I might end up in court after all, but on the wrong side. Seems more likely, anyhow. I don't know anyone from Bryant Street who's ever turned into a lawyer, but I know plenty of folks behind bars.

CHAPTER 24

I RETURN TO THE APARTMENT TO FIND MAMA AND Raheem hunched over the kitchen table with their heads together.

"We don't have to worry about that yet," Mama's saying. "There's a grace period."

"No, look. It's already past due," Raheem says. "We have to pay them something by the end of the month."

"Rent comes first," Mama says. "It's all we have enough for. And we have to eat."

"I know, but we have to . . ." His voice trails off as Mama gets up from the table. Or else as he sees me coming over. Stifling whatever was left to say, he folds the household bills into a neat stack.

"Hey, Maxie."

"Are we in trouble again?" I ask. Raheem gives me the shut-your-mouth look. The one that makes him seem all grown-up and the only thing it makes me want to do in response is stick out my tongue at him. He rolls his eyes.

"Don't worry your head about it," Mama says. She fills a cup of water from the tap. Looks at me over the rim as she sips.

I do worry about it. I don't know why they try to hide it from me. I can always tell when we're broke.

Raheem gets up from the table and puts the bills in the cupboard where we hide them when we don't want to think about the reality of things. "I have to go. I have a shift."

"At work?" I say.

He catches my eye. "Policing."

Mama lets her cup clatter onto the counter. "They pay you for that?"

Raheem gives me another look, as if to remind me why we try not to talk about Panther stuff in front of Mama too much. "It's important," he tells her.

"Important," she repeats, cutting her eyes to the closed cabinet where the bills are hiding.

Raheem leans heavy on the back of the chair. "A minute ago, you said everything's fine. Is it fine or isn't it?"

After a moment, caught like that, Mama shrugs. "You go do whatever you gotta do."

"Yeah, I will." Raheem sweeps past me, grabbing up his black jacket on the way out of the apartment.

Mama serves me fried eggs with rice and beans for dinner. The combo is good. The volume is small. I look at the sack of uncooked rice on the counter and wonder how far we'll have to stretch it.

My imagination strays to the full plate of food I'll get tomorrow at The Breakfast, but I'm careful not to mention it to Mama.

"How's school?" she says. I find this troubling.

"Same as always."

"You like your teachers? You got any grades to show me yet?" Troubling because she's coming down from the place she likes to live, where the things we do to be real in the world—like turn in homework and pay bills on time— don't matter.

"A-minus on a math test," I tell her. "Not too shabby."

"You're a smart girl." She smiles at me.

I duck my head, proud. "Maybe."

"You're both smart." She looks at the door like Raheem is just beyond it. "I don't know where that comes from."

"Oh, Mama."

"I tell people," she says. "I ain't much, but I done two things good."

"Sure. You do a lot of good stuff. You're a good person." I should say more, maybe.

She looks at me across our small empty bowls. I pick them up and take them to the sink. We've all but licked them clean. I barely have to rinse them; the soap is just a formality.

"I'm going out for a while," she says, over the sound of the water running. I know this tone of voice, the voice that comes when the bill pile is high and the only thing that'll make it better is to get away for a while. To the bar, to the liquor store, to some guy we haven't met yet, probably don't want to.

I shut off the tap. Don't bother to look over my shoulder. "Where to?"

If she answers I don't hear it. Just footsteps on the floor and the door closing quietly.

Raheem comes home late from policing, seems surprised to find me lying on the couch instead of gone to bed.

"Where's Mama?"

"Out."

Raheem studies me for a second. Then he goes to the cabinet and brings out the bills. I've left all the lights off, except the one lamp that stands between the end of the kitchen counter and the back of the living room chair. Tipping the pile toward the lamplight, he flips the papers one by one and sighs. He picks a paper from the pile, puts the rest back. He takes the coffee can down and counts out the money inside, adds a few dollars from his pocket and attaches it to the bill with a paperclip. He folds it into his pocket, to be taken down to some office and paid in the morning.

"Is it bad?" I ask.

"Just a rough patch," he says. "Honestly."

"Okay."

Raheem comes and stands near me, his shins against the small square coffee table. His body blocks the lamplight, looming over me in shadow. "You know I'm gonna take care of you, right?"

My breath leaves me softly. "Yeah."

I can see only his outline. I don't know what he can see of me. My furrowed brow, or the way my fingers are laced so tight across my stomach. He does take care of me. If it wasn't for Raheem, Mama would have slid into nothingness by now, and surely dragged me with her. But no matter how he tries to make it seem okay, often it feels like we're still sliding.

CHAPTER 25

OST DAYS AROUND THE NEIGHBOR-
hood nothing changes. As summer tips
toward fall, the weather starts its slow tilt
coldward.

I've realized now that Sam has good days and bad days.
On the good days he wants to talk and do things. On the
bad days he just wants to hold my hand and walk. More
often than not, I let him. But things still have to get done.

Today we head toward the Panther office together. He
rests his arm across my shoulders and I think about things
like kissing. My arm goes around his waist and suddenly
we take a little detour.

Sam leads me into the narrow alley between Charlie's
Soda and the check-cashing place. We know from the past
that if you go far enough in, beyond the Dumpster, the garbage smell goes away and it's just nice and quiet.

We sit on castaway milk crates. He holds my face in his

hands and kisses me. My arms around his back. His hands on my waist. Kissing. Kissing. After a while he's leaning me back against the bales of flattened cardboard at an awkward angle.

"Wait—" I put my hands on his shoulders.

He gives me this misty-eyed stare. "Come on."

"Come on, what?" I wet my lips. He watches. Leans back in.

I hold his shoulders, force him to look at me.

"It's the only thing that feels good," he whispers.

"I know." I let up, let his lips meet mine again. It erases the world around us. The slight garbage stench, the pressures of the neighborhood, the memories of Steve.

No words. No plan. Just what feels right.

Which is exactly what makes it all wrong.

"Stop."

He does, drawing away from me altogether.

"What are we doing?" I ask him. "I mean—"

"Let's go to the office," he says, standing up and starting down the alley.

I swallow. "What?"

He's halfway to the Dumpster already, leaving me behind. I'm stunned motionless.

"Can that actually happen?" I blurt. "Can you just start kissing me and then act like it never happened?"

Sam doesn't say anything or even look back. If it seemed like a good day at first, it's a bad day now.

Sam beats me to the office by better than half a block. I, for one, am walking slower because I feel the need to pull myself together. Mainly so I don't make a fool of both of us by blowing up at him in front of the whole office.

I see him go in the door, and by the time I get there he's already disappeared into the back room. So be it. I flop into one of the desk chairs.

Rocco hefts a twine-bound stack of newspapers onto the desk in front of me. I hand him scissors from the drawer and he slices the bundle open. Says, "You got a copy of the new issue yet?"

"No."

"You got a quarter?"

I shake my head.

"Okay." He reaches into his pocket and pulls one out. Lays it on the table between us. "You try and pay me back if you can, okay?"

"Sure."

Rocco picks up the paper and opens it to about the middle. He takes the scissors from the desk and carefully cuts out a big corner. Spins it and spreads it with his fingers so I can see.

"Read this," he tells me. "Tell me if there's anything you don't understand."

"Okay." I reach for it. Start to slip it into my school bag.

"No, read it now. Then you got to fold it in your pocket. Every day, all the time. You feel me?"

Rocco folds the rest of the paper neat while I struggle with the words on the page.

The Pocket Lawyer of Legal First Aid:
What you need to know if you are arrested.

1. Remain silent.

2. Do not resist arrest.

There are fourteen points on the list. It's going to take me a long time to get through it, and Rocco's sitting there waiting.

I take the rest of the paper and tuck it under my arm. "Okay, I get it," I tell him.

"You sure?" Rocco pats his pocket. "I got mine right here."

"Thanks. I'll pay you back." There's usually some way to get a touch of spare change. Anyway, the other day Leroy was talking about how buying the paper is an investment, in knowledge and awareness. I guess he meant it's not like buying an ice cream, because you don't just enjoy it for a minute. It lasts.

Sam emerges from the back room, comes over to us. He catches me with his sad eyes and it makes me wish he would just come out and say whatever it is that he's holding behind them.

"Hey, man." Rocco drums his fingers on the desk. "I'm headed over to the clinic in a minute. You want a ride there?"

"Naw, I'll walk," Sam says. "Stuff to do around here first."

"No hurry. I'll wait for you."

"No," Sam says, kind of sharp.

"He has to walk me home too," I say, trying to cover. Sam won't ride in a car anymore unless it's absolutely necessary. It's because Steve died in a car; he was sitting in the passenger seat, in fact, when he was shot to death by some cops that pulled them over. Raheem was driving; Sam was in the back. He saw it all happen. No way to erase a memory like that. Raheem told me it's the worst thing he's ever witnessed in life, and after where we come from, that's saying something. It must go double for Sam. I tried for a long time to get him past the things he sees when the door closes behind us. When the brakes ease on and he clenches his eyes like it's happening all over and over. I'd hold his hand, but nothing doing.

I should know, things like that have a way of coming back, even when the worst and more has already happened and every last tear has been squeezed out of you.

CHAPTER 26

UTIFULLY SAM WALKS ME HOME. HE'S not happy about it, mainly because my frustration with him is manifesting as a whole bunch of chatter. I like kissing Sam, but I used to like talking to him too. I want to be able to do that.

I can't stop myself, and he's not filling in his side of things, so I'm coming across as something of a runaway train.

"You wanna go down to the water?" It's my last-ditch effort to have something actually happen here.

Sam turns his wrist to get a look at his watch. "I have to be home," he says. "Dinner."

"Oh." I wonder what it feels like to be tied to a place and time like that. Sounds like a drag to me, but maybe it's nice knowing someone will miss you if you don't show up when you're supposed to. I come and go as I please.

We say good night on my sidewalk, as usual. No kiss.

No hand-holding. No lingering or last words. Just this strange new distance between us.

I climb up and up and slip inside the apartment, thinking about supper and maybe a little bit of Panther reading before bedtime. Maybe try to figure out the list Rocco gave me. But I pause in the doorway, unsettled by something out of sight. It's quiet at home, but not the calm sort of quiet. Then I see them.

A large pair of work shoes tangled with Mama's black pumps, just beside the door.

I ache with disappointment. It's been a while since Mama tried on a man for size. A long enough while to make me almost forget the bad times.

No. I'll never forget. But it's been long enough to start me believing it might never happen again.

There have been men before. Twelve men in maybe eight years, starting from the time the main man up and walked out on us. Some stay longer than others. The ones I like never stay long enough. He wasn't the best of them, my real dad, but he's the only one I miss.

"*He's a good man, baby. It's going to be different this time.*" She's usually right about things being different, but almost never right about him being good. Least not good enough for us.

It's almost always the shoes I see first. Sometimes it's the voices. The moment she lets them into the place, into her bed, it begins. The roughness around the house that keeps me on edge, keeps me on the street until the last possible second.

It was just the one who tried to touch me, before I learned to live on edge. One hit Raheem, and one hit Ma and that was that for each of those. Most of the rest were no-good suckers too, but least they kept their hands to themselves. Two were nice enough. One I liked, woulda had him stay forever was it up to me, but now I don't let myself even think his name. You can't walk back to the good past neither. Once you learn how to be putting things behind, it's all or nothing.

Sliding back into the hall, I close the door again. Real quiet, like I hadn't even been there.

C H A P T E R **27**

I WANDER DOWN TO THE CORNER STORE AND hang by the snack counter, hoping old Clem will take pity on me and give me a taste of something. He's a softie, as long as you don't take advantage and try to play him too often. A new-man day isn't exactly special, but it's the sort of thing that makes me want to treat myself.

Twenty minutes of sad eyes does the trick. Clem gives me a beef patty and a grape soda, which ought to keep my belly happy. No way to know what will happen about dinner, since Mama seems otherwise engaged. Then I walk a long figure eight around the blocks, chewing and sipping as I go. Could go to the park, I guess, but I just feel like walking and thinking. It'd help if I could remember Raheem's exact work schedule for today and what time he's likely to get home.

There's a darkness to these buildings, even in daylight, but it stands out especially at sunset. Before the lights go on indoors and things begin to glow and it's clear that the day is over. At dusk, the street takes on a restless insomnia, a heavy-lidded stumbling toward the night. The furtive underbelly of things, all pale and hairy, pokes through to the surface.

Mama tries hard to do right by us, but in the end she wants not to be alone. Raheem and I aren't enough for her, it seems. Four is better, she told me once, but that isn't always true. My real dad is never coming back, we're pretty sure, and that's the only thing that could ever put it right. I don't get my hopes up anymore.

I like to stroll at this time of day, when everyone else wants to be in. Emmalee says I'm the sort of person who can't be confined, which I like because it makes me sound larger than life. I'm only fourteen, but I've seen things, known them. I had a first kiss and a second one, felt a boy's tongue against mine. Sam's lips, all big and soft and curious. I know how nice it is to have someone's hand to hold, instead of walking all alone. Can't really blame Mama for wanting that.

No matter how much I want to, I can't stay out all night. The sky gets dark and there always comes a moment when it's time to go home. I think about going to stay at Emmalee's instead, but you never really know what you're gonna find there, either.

I slip through the door. He's sitting on the couch, big as life. Mama lying with her head on his thigh. He's skinny, looking like a stiff breeze off the lake would bend him in the middle. Salt-and-pepper hair, scrag of a beard. Wearing an undershirt over tan pants. Bare feet on the rug.

"My daughter," she says to him as I enter. "Maxie, this is Wil."

"Oh," I say.

He returns my cool gaze with one of his own. "Nice to meet you, Maxie."

He gets a point for actually saying my name, but that's about all I can give him. I ignore the fact that he's spoken to me, and retreat to my room for the night.

CHAPTER 28

WITH WIL COMING AROUND MOST evenings, I make a point of staying out all afternoon until I'm sure Mama's going to be home. I don't want him coming by, catching me alone. Expecting to be let in to wait. Being out is what I do anyway, but when it feels necessary like this, it's sometimes harder to find things to do to fill the time.

Emmalee's gone off to do her homework and Patrice is nowhere to be found. There's plenty going on at the playground, but I'm not in the mood for any of it, so I skirt the park. Decide to take a walk instead. I'm thinking of going to the clinic to see what Sam is up to. It's the very thing Emmalee and Patrice talk me out of doing on a day-to-day basis, but when they're not around I forget all the reasons why I'm supposed to leave Sam alone.

I'm headed that way when the mood in the street suddenly changes. Just ahead of me, a shop door clatters open with little bells. Cherry steps out into the street, wearing one of her painted-on dresses. She pauses to light a cigarette. The guys hanging on the stoops start looking over their shoulders and nudging each other that way that they do.

Cherry's body talks and the men around her listen. The sway of her hips is something magical. She glides along the sidewalk and their heads turn like clockwork. Half a block behind, I try to copy her moves—the way her arm dangles over her handbag and the free wrist dances, flicking the ash of her cigarette. For a few seconds I become another kind of girl—no, woman—the kind who can't and won't be left behind by maturity or love or anything unnamed.

"Maxie?" Rocco says. "You okay, girl?"

He steps out of the convenience store, landing a couple of paces ahead of me. I roll around toward him, hand on my tilted hip. "Hi, Rocco."

"You look dizzy. Is it the heat? You need a drink?"

"You buying?" I go for a low, husky, sexy voice.

"Grab a Coke on me," Rocco says, frowning. He extends two fingers toward me, a quarter trapped between. "You sound like you might be coming down with something."

I straighten up, real casual, hoping there's no color giving away the warmth that flushes my cheeks. But I guess he'd only mistake it for a fever. I take the quarter and run inside.

The cool Coke hits the spot. When I step back onto the sidewalk, Rocco's gone. So is Cherry, but I try the thing with my hips again anyway. What I need are shoes with a heel, I think. They add a little something extra.

I sashay my way down to the Panther office, wondering if I'll find Cherry there. Sure enough, when I pop in the door, she's got her hips propped on the desk nearest the window, chatting up Slim, who's sitting at the desk and looking up at her like a fool grinning straight into the sunshine.

"Hi, Maxie," Cherry says.

"Hey, sister," Slim says, but his gaze is slipping toward Cherry's southern real estate.

"Hi." I glide by them, straight to my usual station, where a large stack of envelopes and sheets of stamps sit waiting. I wet a sponge in the kitchen and set to work sealing and stamping.

Leroy, Jolene, Hamlin, and Lester are midconversation, gathered around the couch area. "All I'm saying is it's a growing problem in Oakland," Hamlin says. "There's always someone willing to take a payoff to pass on information. Especially when it seems like small things that won't hurt anybody."

"What's your point?" Leroy says.

"The point is, it's a slippery slope. Information is power. Tidbits matter."

"We get that," Jolene says. "So what are they doing about it?"

"That's the thing," Hamlin says. "They're not sure what to do. It's not only the leaks. There's also significant misinformation coming back into the ranks from the informants. Trying to confuse things."

"I want to keep talking about this," Leroy says with a sigh. "But I have calls to make."

"Maxie can do it," Jolene says.

My ears perk up. I set aside the sopping sponge.

Leroy looks over his shoulder. "Okay. Maxie." He hands me a scrap of paper with phone numbers written on it. "Call these people and confirm that their food donations for The Breakfast are arriving sometime tomorrow."

"Sure."

I like to use the phone. The big black receiver is weighty in my hand. I imagine it holding all the words ever spoken through it, and all the ones to come. My finger slides into the holes, one by one, dialing the plate around. There are two sevens, two nines, and a zero involved, which means the dial spins all the way around most of the time. Click, click, click, click. Whee.

C H A P T E R **29**

'M WALKING HOME, STILL HIGH ON THE EFFECTS of talking on the phone. If I ever get a real office job, I can have a phone of my own, right on my very desk. I can pick it up and dial it anytime I want, for important business or just to see who answers. I like the idea of that. It has me skipping down the street.

I should know by now — good feelings only last so long.

Emmalee dashes toward me, that look of flight in her eyes that I know so well. I put out my hand to receive her.

Emmalee's cool fingers grip mine. "I don't want to go home tonight," she says.

"It's okay."

I've been at her place when her dad comes home in a messed-up mood. The best thing to do is always to remove ourselves from the picture.

We link arms and walk quickly, away from our familiar doorways, around the corner. I lean into her in a way that says "I know," at least I hope it does. It's different for me, but I know how it feels to need to run.

"Do you want to look for Patrice?" I offer. Patrice with her quiet mother. Her father, who has a steady job and doesn't raise his voice unless we earn it. Patrice with a bed wide enough for the three of us, and a room all to herself. We smile at her parents and call it a sleepover, but most times it's really something else.

Emmalee shakes her head. "Please. I can't."

I get it. Sometimes it's too hard to smile, in the face of everything we lack. Patrice loves us, struggles with us, but there are some things she really can't see.

"Okay, then." We circle the block, arm in arm. As if one slow turn might change what it is we'll return to.

CHAPTER 30

EMMALEE'S GOING TO SLEEP OVER," I announce to Ma and Wil. They're coiled on the living room sofa, staring at some static snow on the television. I can't even tell what show's on underneath.

"It's a school night," Mama says. "Did you do your homework?"

"We're going to finish it now," I tell her. Emmalee doesn't have her books over here, but we can make do with mine. It's all the same.

Turns out Emmalee's already done her homework. She's smart like that. Gets good grades, way better than mine. She makes me read to her the assignment out of the history book before she lets me skip to the math.

"Haven't you read it already?" I say.

"Yeah, but have you?" Emmalee's going to be a teacher when she grows up. She already knows how to do that look they do that tells you to hush, you're supposed to be working. It comes as easy to her as a smile. Going to college, then being a teacher. That's her big dream. She doesn't come out and say it ever, but it's one of those things we just know.

Raheem slides in and sees Emmalee. "Again?"

"Shut up," I tell him. "She's staying."

"I didn't mean it like that." A fierce expression passes over Raheem's face. "One of these days," he says, then draws the curtain.

Emmalee lays her head on my shoulder. "He's nice," she whispers. "Wanting to do something."

"Yeah." But we both know he won't. Can't. It's not like us, where the guys come and go. Emmalee's dad is her dad, and that's that.

I click off my lamp. Raheem puts his on, so there's a soft glow in the room. It's how I like to fall asleep most nights. Knowing he's over there. In the not-quite-dark.

Best of all is Emmalee's quiet presence. The whispers of her breath. We snuggle down under the covers and don't even touch, but she's right there with me.

I wake slightly trembling. Remnants of a nightmare. Things chasing me. White- and brown-skinned men with erased faces. Bucky Willis, all bloody. Steve Childs, shot full of holes and sinking into a rectangle plot of earth. There was a fair amount of screaming, in my head. I breathe hard to draw myself out of the dream space.

Emmalee's limbs spider over me. I pluck them one by one and slide from beneath the sheets. I sit on the edge of the bed for a while, looking at the curtain, listening to Raheem and Emmalee breathing in off-kilter rhythms.

The dream has left me mind sick, heartsick, belly sick. A storm of icky feelings.

When I lie back down, Emmalee automatically rolls to hug me in her sleep. Her arms coil around one of mine, the way I might hold Little Ralphie, who is tucked safe in his drawer at the moment. Her cheek touches my shoulder.

I'm glad she's here. I'm glad not to be so alone, but I can't make myself close my eyes. I study the spots on the ceiling, wondering if sleep will hit me by accident between now and when the sun comes up.

CHAPTER 31

I ARRIVE LATE TO POLITICAL EDUCATION CLASS because I've been all the way on the other side of the neighborhood, putting up flyers for the health clinic. When I slip in the door, it appears as if all hell has broken loose.

"Guns, shoot!" someone yells out. "Y'all cowards when it comes down to it. Ain't no one gonna ever pull a trigger?"

"All police are pigs!" someone else shouts over the din.

"No," Leroy says sharply, cutting through the stew of voices. "We respect police officers who respect us."

"They just happen to be few and far between," Hamlin calls out.

"I ain't never met one!" Gumbo tosses in. People chuckle.

"I hear that," Leroy says. "But you've also got to understand the principle. We defend ourselves against actions that are unjust. Cop tries to cuff you, let him cuff you. But if the cop tries to beat you, pull your gun and hope he backs off. See the difference?"

"I ain't getting cuffed for no crime I didn't commit," Gumbo declares.

Leroy shakes his head. "That's what the legal defense fund is for. We don't resist arrest, rightful or wrongful. We do resist brutality. We need to show them we respect the law, but won't stand for them stepping outside of it. You dig?"

"What's going on?" I whisper, sidling up beside Sam, who's standing in the back. Possibly waiting for me. I hope.

"Oh, they saw someone get picked up during policing rounds today. People don't understand why the Panthers let him get arrested."

"The cops beat on him?" I think of Bucky.

"No, he just got collared for stealing batteries out of the corner store."

"Did he do it?"

Sam shrugs. "No idea. The point is, it was a lawful arrest, so the Panther policers had to let it go. On principle."

"And some people want blood anyway," I say, looking around at the couple of people who are still leaping out of their seats, shouting out that the Panthers are cowards.

"Off the pigs!" someone yells.

Sam nods. That's the way it goes, I guess. There are always some people who want blood. Maybe it's the same people who always end up ripping up storefronts during riots, people who think doing anything is better than doing nothing and don't care about doing it smart.

Tonight Raheem is one of the guys at the edges of the room, all suited up and with shotguns. He's standing between Lester and Slim. I wave and he nods.

Eventually Leroy regains control of the audience. "Okay," he says. "We're going off script. Let's talk Self-Defense Theory 101. Answer me this—Why do Panthers pack guns?"

"To off the pigs!" someone shouts from the back. The whole class murmurs in agreement, a rolling wave of angry whispers.

"Wrong," Leroy says. "Why do Panthers pack guns?"

Hamlin calls out, "Because the Second Amendment of the United States Constitution entitles citizens to defend themselves and their homes and their families against tyranny."

"Correct," Leroy says. "We're citizens, and for us the tyranny isn't coming from outside; it's coming from our country itself. Why else?"

"Because when we're stripped of our rights, as black people have been for centuries in America, they start to see us as less than human," Gumbo says.

"And?"

"And then they treat us like we're less than human."

"And?"

"And now we have to remind them."

Leroy nods. "Because we need them to know we won't stand for it anymore," he says. "We won't stand for what happened to Bucky Willis. We won't stand for what happened to Steve Childs."

Beside me, Sam flinches. I reach for his hand.

"The pigs know we are watching," Leroy says. "We're watching, we're listening, and we're taking a stand."

C H A P T E R **3 2**

'VE SEALED SO MANY ENVELOPES THAT I THINK the sponge has molded to the shape of my palm. The door to the office is propped open to let in a breeze. The muggy summer weather has cooled to early fall pleasantness, but the air in here is still warm.

Jolene sits at the typewriter churning out letter after letter, and I fold each and every one and put it in an envelope ready to mail. Leroy's making phone calls. Rocco and Slim are hanging on the sofa, waiting to lay some knowledge on anyone who walks in.

A good thing about being here all the time is that I always get the skinny on everything. No one really notices me when I keep my head down and stay on task, so I hear it all.

First, it's Cherry. She comes in dressed in a tight skirt and bangles and gets up in Leroy's face. "Give me a shift," she says. "I'm tired of this newspaper-selling bull." She slams a sack of coins on the desktop.

"Come on, Cherry," Leroy argues. He picks up the money. "You bring in more cash than anyone."

"So?" she snaps. "Someone else can look good standing on a street corner. I've done my training and I want a shift policing."

"You'll get a shift," Leroy says. "But we can use the cash."

Cherry crosses her arms. "I'm not selling another paper until I get a shift."

There's a silence. Leroy looks at Jolene like she's going to bail him out, but she just keeps on pecking the keys like she don't even notice him. Oh, snap. She's on Cherry's side in this one.

"You can come out with us," Rocco says after a moment. "You can trade off with Raheem and Gumbo. They have to cut out for their regular jobs a lot."

Cherry tosses him a look. Maybe a little grateful, but also a little annoyed. Like she wanted it to come from Leroy. "Great," she says. "When?"

Rocco shrugs. "I think Raheem is working tomorrow. The afternoon/evening shift."

"Fine. See you then." Cherry flounces out, gracing Leroy with a last glare as she goes on her way.

Leroy turns to Rocco. "I don't think she's ready."

Rocco shrugs. "It was gonna be just the two of us tomorrow. Everyone's working."

"You really want to sit in a car with her for six hours?"

Slim grins ear to ear. "I sure do."

"We all know you do," Jolene snaps. "And Cherry will be fine."

Hamlin comes in a few minutes later. He calls a small side meeting with Leroy, drawing him to the front desk, where I suppose he imagines they are out of earshot. Maybe he's right. Jolene's keys click loudly; Slim and Rocco are chatting up some new guy who strolled in wanting to join up. But my ears are honed.

"I followed up about the talk we had during the convention," Hamlin says. "Bobby says they're having some trouble with informants in Oakland. Pigs paying people off to report on what the Panthers are doing."

"You thinking we should be worried?"

"I'm thinking we should be careful who we let in new."

Leroy shrugs. "Everyone wants in after the convention mess. Can't stop people from joining. How we going to screen for that?"

"Pigs are always gonna have their ways."

"Exactly."

"We just gotta let everybody know the punishment for traitors is—" Hamlin draws a finger sharply across his throat. "Once that's out there, people might think twice about messing with us."

CHAPTER 33

LIKE HOW IT WORKED OUT FOR CHERRY WHEN she came in and told Leroy straight up how she wanted things to go. But Leroy knows I screwed up on the quarters. I don't know if anything I've done since then can make up for it.

Instead, I try talking to Jolene. "I want to do more," I tell her. "I want to go to Panther training." Raheem has been, and Sam is going, along with most of the other guys I know. I don't want to get left any further behind.

"You'll go when you're older, Maxie," Jolene says, handing me the letters. "What you do around here helps too."

"It's boring," I confess.

"Honey, it's work. Trust me, you'd get just as bored of policing after a while."

Somehow I find that hard to believe. There's danger out there on the street, riding in the wake of the cops. You have to keep on your toes. Get to be a hero sometimes. That doesn't sound boring at all.

"No," I start to say. But Sam comes in the door right then, followed by a couple of guys I recognize from the clinic. I know he sees me, because his gaze passes through mine, but then he sweeps right along into the back room with the others. No greeting at all. Not so much as a second glance.

It confuses me when he turns so cold. Moments like this make it true what the girls always say, that Sam only makes me want to hide away and cry. It adds to my feelings of wanting to run, wanting to fight. It makes me want to pound the desk, mad that I still look for him, still want to talk to him and walk with him. I don't know why I can't forget him.

I try to shove Sam out of my mind, try to stop my voice from breaking. "Please," I tell Jolene. "I'm ready to start now."

"There is something we need done, Maxie," Leroy says. I spin around, because I didn't see him come over or realize he overheard anything I was saying.

"What?" It comes out breathless. "I can do it. I can do anything."

"The youth classes have been looking a little lean the last few Saturdays," he says. "You know the neighborhood kids. Make some rounds and get them over to The Breakfast and the Freedom School."

The little girls turning double Dutch on the flat concrete playground watch us approach out the corners of their eyes. I can see them peeking more, the closer we get. Probably think we're coming to cause trouble. Some of the older kids like to mess with them. I remember how it was.

The watching girls exchange glances and, almost as one, start chanting, cheering on the girl skipping ropes. "Go Lizzie. Go Lizzie."

Solidarity, sisters. I smile, try to look friendly.

"Can we join?" Emmalee says. They giggle.

Shenelle Willis, Bucky's little sister, is one of the girls turning the ropes. "Are you any good?"

Emmalee fixes a look on her that might have frozen the ropes in the air. "Girl, we were skipping before you were born."

"Don't mean you're no good," pants Lizzie, leaping out of the center. The girls keep turning. The empty ropes slap the concrete. These girls really know how to turn. The rhythm is perfect—it rocks something within me, lulls me back to the time when this was all there was in the world for me.

Emmalee and I look at each other. It has been a minute since we did this, but I can feel it all coming back. We shrug off our book bags, roll our shoulders to loosen up.

"Ready?" I say.

Shenelle grins. "Yeah." They open their arms, creating a larger pocket within the ropes. Emmalee is taller than any of them, plus there's two of us going in.

Emmalee rocks to catch the rhythm. We had a bunch of routines together back in the day, but only a few we came to consider classic. I can tell by the way she's standing which one we're starting in on. I turn my back, wait till I hear her rhythmic footfalls, then leap between the ropes to join her.

We're jumping back to back for what feels like an eternity before Emmalee cues me to start the turns. All she does is suck in a breath in this certain way, and I know it's time. Sure as the sunrise. To this day, it's our little secret, something we stumbled upon by chance. No one could ever figure out how we both knew to turn at the same time.

This routine is our most impressive-looking, when it goes right. I concentrate hard on the timing. Hop in a circle, hop in a circle. Hop half a circle. Hands, clap. Hop in a circle, quarter turn, stop. Reverse. One hand slap. Quarter turn, stop. Reverse. Quarter turn, quarter turn, quarter turn, stop. Hop in a circle, double hand clap. Double spin, double spin, double spin. Jump! Regular rhythm. Hands clap. Hop turn, hop turn, hop turn, slap.

Yes! Our right hands clasped, we face each other, breathing hard. Jumping. The little girls cheer around us.

We tighten our grip for the grand finale. Emmalee breathes and whoosh! We pull each other's hands, switch places. Jump a moment longer, back to back. Leap out on opposite sides. We dismount with our fists in the air, triumphant.

Shenelle and the other girl stop turning. They cluster toward us. "Whoa, how'd you do that spin?"

"I want to learn to switch places!"

"Can you show us?"

"Sure," Emmalee says. "Most of it isn't that hard, once you know the ropes real well."

I hang back and let her do her thing. I learned most of what I know about jumping from her to begin with.

Across the yard, Sam and Rocco chat up some boys around the basketball hoop. I watch them for a minute as Emmalee doles out double Dutch tips. Rocco's right in the thick of it, switching off with a couple of guys shooting free throws in turn. Sam's leaning against the half wall, talking with two boys on the sidelines. Not even once does he look my way.

I hate the uncertainty of us these days. The way he brushed by me earlier without so much as a hi. I hate not knowing what it means, or what to do.

Emmalee nudges me. "Come on, Max, let's turn for them."

"Sure." I take the ropes in my hand. They settle in my

palm. I've always preferred ropes like these, that don't have handles. The thick gray cord loops around my fingers, familiar as yesterday. Emmalee sets the rhythm. My arms just follow, falling into place like they always did. It feels good, being back here. It feels lighter. I try to free my mind from the weight of things, and it almost kind of works.

But the little girls try all our fancy spins. Get tangled, time and again. They're learning. I know better than to be annoyed with them, but I can't help it. I just want to stand here, just want to turn and let the rhythm carry me away. I say things like "Good try. Turn your foot out a little more," but I feel my voice growing tighter. I think Emmalee can sense it in me. She gathers her rope ends in one hand. Nods to me.

"Tomorrow's Saturday," I tell the girls. "If you come to The Breakfast, the Panthers are going to have some stuff for us to do afterward. Will you come?"

They erupt in a chorus of "Yes!"

We hand back the ropes. "See you then!"

C H A P T E R 3 4

E MMALEE TRIES TO TALK ME OUT OF WHAT I'm headed to do. I don't bother to wonder how she can read me so easily. I'm making a beeline for Sam and I'm sure it's transparent.

"Sam." He's moving away, almost running. Not actually running, though I nearly have to in order to keep up.

"I have to go."

"No, wait."

"I'll see you tomorrow, Maxie."

He streaks away, which only ticks me off. Sam's supposed to be the steady one; it's me who can't sit still.

"I wouldn't kiss you *one time* and so now you're ignoring me? That's low," I shout after him. But he let me hold his hand at the meeting the other night, so none of it makes any sense.

Emmalee comes up behind me. She takes my arm, tries to turn me around. "Let it go. You're supposed to be getting over him, remember?"

Sometimes the pep talk works; sometimes it doesn't. We all know I'm not over him. Shaking her loose, I chase after Sam, tailing him all the way down toward the water. "Stop. Why won't you walk with me?"

"Leave me alone, Maxie."

I know I should. Of course I should, but I can't. "I want to talk to you."

"Not today," he snaps.

"It kind of feels like that means never."

He spins on me and the look on his face actually makes me take a step back, like maybe he's about to hit me. "Not today."

"Why not?"

"Not today!" he screams, and it's the kind of rage that makes a girl end up with bruises, but I can't believe it of him so I press.

"Why not?"

His eyes glow with that certain light, that my-way-or-the-highway light that I've seen before, and I brace myself. Because if it's going to happen, it has to be now, so I can stop believing he's different.

He moves his hands. It's only the smallest movement, but I flinch.

It's quick. A reflex. I can't help it.

Sam freezes. His gentle hands hang there, inches from mine, stuck like he knows I'm afraid. But I'm not anymore.

All the air goes out of him, and the fight, and the spirit.

I put out my hand. Ashamed of thinking even for a second that Sam would ever in the world try to harm me.

"I'm sorry," he says, drawing his fingers back, away. "You should go."

"Sam–"

He covers his face with his hands. A small gnawing ache twists low in my belly. Something's happening, outside of me, outside of us, to him alone. I begin to feel it, not knowing why I haven't sensed it all along.

"Get away from me," he says. "I'm no good right now. Just leave."

A cool wind sweeps off the water, forcing its way between us.

I press the words out, arcing them across the invisible divide. "I'm not going," I promise. "Just tell me."

The silence stretches long, but he doesn't move away again. He lowers his hands and the air seems to sting his eyes. When he blinks they overflow.

"It's his birthday," he murmurs.

The wind whips at the words, wraps around us and catches us. As good as naked in this moment, me figuring everything out.

"I didn't know."

Sam turns and walks to the edge of the water. He might

as well have drifted away, for all there is left to touch of him. I don't even know whether to try or not.

Across the water the clouds bunch up along the horizon, moving away from us. A great storm brewing in the distance. I long for it to crash over us, to wash us clean. To give us something to listen to besides the blur of traffic in the empty echo air and our own hearts beating, where Steve's is not and never will again.

Sam kicks off his shoes and wades in until his pants are wet to the knees. I follow. My toes slide into the gritty sand. The water laps mindlessly, seizing my skin like ice. My skirt hem catches the tips of the waves, and the spill of the tide draws my mind back to the day it happened.

He'd come to the water that day too, tried to lose himself in the lake, I don't know, or tried to lull his mind toward forgetting.

There can be no forgetting. We know that, and that's why it hurts. I slide my hand into his and put my cheek on his sleeve at the shoulder. He's grown taller now. I lift my head for a second to know for sure and, yes, I can tuck myself right under his chin. So I do. Wrap my arms around his waist, glue myself to his chest, and hold him while the tears rain down.

We hug long and quiet in the wind and the water, and I can feel him choking on memories. Swallow some of my own. I can feel how he carries it with him, this ache, but there's nothing I can do to erase it.

His hands move on the skin of my arms, setting me away at last. I kiss his mouth and brush the wet streaks from his cheeks. In the depths of his eyes I spy the storm I had wished for, and it isn't about to pass.

CHAPTER 35

WE WALK HAND IN HAND FOR A long while after that. Along the water, along the streets, through the park, and back. We don't talk or anything, which is okay at first, but then I start thinking maybe the good-girlfriend thing to do would be to chatter and take his mind off things. Except all my thoughts are the kind that would make things worse. I think about Steve and how he used to smile when he saw me coming, and how he always talked about Sam to me like he was trying to sell me a car. I think about Raheem and how most days he drives me to the point where I want to wring his thick old neck, yet I can't imagine the world existing without him. He's like a brick wall between me and everything out there that wants me, the good, the bad, all of it. Sure, I spend my days trying to chip it down, but if it really fell, I'd feel, I don't know, exposed. So I keep my big mouth shut. Sam squeezes my fingers time and again. I search my heart for the right thing to say in the face of the sadness, but it's never that easy, and the air grows cold.

Maybe I ought to walk Sam home, but we do it the other way around, like usual. He leaves me at my door and walks away with his head hanging. I don't want to go inside, because I never want to go inside, so I stand looking after him. Thinking about all the times he's left me here with a kiss still tingling on my lips while he spins away, smiling. Wondering if, when he walks away, he ever feels any piece of my dread or knows that the worst part of my day is ahead. I'll never understand his pain, but at least I see it. I reach out and touch it, because he lets me. Would he ever know . . . ever be able to do the same for me?

CHAPTER 36

THE APARTMENT DOOR OPENS, LIKE HE knows I'm there.

"Heya, Maxie."

"Wil."

He spells it with one *L*, he told me, because he's Wilbur. Not William or something usual. What kind of name is Wilbur for a skinny old city brother, I want to know, but these are things I don't bring up.

He pulls a folded buck out his pocket, shows it to me. "Going for smokes."

"Right on." I step aside, all smooth and easy, hoping he'll take the hint. *I'll stay out of your way, you stay the hell out of mine.*

He nods, one of those chin-raising what-up kind of deals, and moves on down the hall. So far I don't have a problem with Wil. He's my kind of conversationalist.

Ma's inside, all laid out on the couch, trying to play like it's the longest day of her life come to the resting place.

"Where've you been?"

"Been where I been." I glide past her, right on into my bedroom. Looking like that, she's not about to follow.

I wake to the sound of Raheem grunting out push-ups on the floor of our room. The curtain is pushed back. Morning light pours in on him, planked out and pumping himself up and down.

"Gross," I say. "You sound like a diseased rhinoceros."

He tips his head up far enough to glare at me. "Girls like pecs."

I snort loudly.

"Now who sounds like wildlife?" he huffs, breathing out the words to the rhythm of his arms.

"Who do you like, anyway?" I try to think if I've seen him getting all mushy on anyone lately.

"Shut up," he grunts.

I stretch out my legs and try to kick him over, but he's pretty well balanced. "You know I'm going to find out. And then I'm going to tell her all about your work-out noises."

"Stop it." He shrugs off my pokes, comes up onto his knees. Then he flips onto his back. Sit-ups.

I come all the way out of bed. "I could stand on your belly. Make it more of a challenge. Girls like abs, too."

My foot dangles over his middle. Raheem grabs my ankle and tugs, making me lose my balance and hop around. "Heem. Heem!" I squeal. He gives me a tiny shove and I flop back onto my mattress.

"That'll teach you to mess with a man and his muscles," Raheem mutters, crunching.

"Don't see no man, don't see no muscles," I quip as I skip out the door to pee.

In the living room Mama has her head out the window. "It's hot out," she says. "Short sleeves, breezy skirt kind of hot."

"That's weird."

I slip into the bathroom, wash my face, brush my teeth.

On my way back through, Mama's in the kitchen eating cereal from the box. Says, "Your brother giving you a hard time? Sounds like you fighting in there."

"Nah."

But back in our room, Raheem is sitting on the edge of the bed, looking mopey.

"She turn you down already?" I joke. "That's fast work."

He looks up at me with this face I don't know what to make of. "What?" I ask. "What happened?"

"Why did you say that before?"

"Say what?"

He squeezes the mattress. "That thing about me not being a man. That's not a nice thing to say."

"You pushed me on the bed."

"I'm a man," he says. "The only man around here. I take care of things."

"I know." He has to get that I was only joking. We do that. We joke.

"Maxie."

Then again, everyone's always telling me how I overrun my mouth. "Come on, you know how I say stuff."

"Yeah. You really gotta stop that."

I shrug. I would if I could help it. Brain. Mouth. There's a superhighway in between. No red lights, no roadblocks.

CHAPTER **37**

THE LATE-OCTOBER HEAT WAVE TAKES everyone by surprise. School is muggy, even with the windows open. Indian summer, my math teacher says, mopping his face with a grungy-looking hankie.

"Let's go swimming," Patrice says after school.

"We have to go to the office," I tell her.

Emmalee throws back her head and sighs. "I'm staying out of it," she says. "We do this every other day."

Patrice and I face off.

"Come on, we might not get to swim again until the summer."

"The Panthers need us. Plus, the harder we work, the more we advance."

"You always think that, and there's never anything to do that we haven't done a million times." Patrice puts on a mocking tone. "Stamp the envelopes. Clean the windows. Make the sandwiches."

Emmalee's right. This conversation is old and tired and I'm starting to ache with it. "Why don't you guys just go without me?"

"Fine, we will," Patrice says.

"Fine." I look at Emmalee, hoping she'll decide to come with me instead.

"Okay," she says, slowly. "Well, maybe we'll stop by the office a little bit later."

"See you." I spin away before she can see my feelings are hurt. It's stupid, anyway. It's not like we've never spent an afternoon apart before. Sometimes I walk with Sam. Sometimes Emmalee goes to Charlie's Soda by herself on days when Jimmy's working. Sometimes Patrice has family stuff. Often, even when we go to the park together, we end up hanging with different people on opposite sides when one thing leads to another.

Behind me, Emmalee and Patrice stroll away, heads close together. I watch them over my shoulder, wondering if they feel, like I do, that today is somehow different.

C H A P T E R 3 8

MIDAFTERNOON AND THE PANTHER OFFICE is cool, with a cross breeze from the propped-open front door and the alley window in the back room. The plate-glass windows are in place, all fresh and shiny. I personally wiped them clean of handprint streaks and dust earlier this week. It brightens up the place to have light streaming in.

Not too many people around right now. We're smack in the lull between the daytime bustle and the evening bustle. Leroy took off about an hour ago for a meeting across town with Fred Hampton. Slim rolled through a few minutes ago, then farmed right back out on a supply run. Lester Smith is napping on the couch.

I've been here awhile. Nowhere else I want to go, really. I've washed the dishes, cleared the desks, put lots of papers into files. All afternoon I've been feeling useful, feeling good. Now there's nothing left to do that I can think of.

Hamlin and Rocco are hunched over a desk drafting some kind of strategy memo, reading each other lines and blurting phrases and echoing each other, taking notes and editing. I hover around them for a while, but I don't really know what they're doing, so after a while it just seems like I'm in the way.

I sit down close to Jolene, watch her calculating numbers with the little adder. It churns out a thick strip of white paper stamped with little gray numbers. The output curls up against the machine. Her right hand rests gracefully arched against the buttons while she traces the lines of the ledger with her left.

"I could read you the numbers," I say. I think I can do it. It's mostly words that trip me up.

"It's okay," she says. "I've got it."

The baby cries from the back room. Jolene glances my way. "Honey, would you get her?"

I slide off the stool. I'm trying to be useful. Every little bit helps, Leroy always says.

Little Betty's raising a medium ruckus by the time I get in there, but she takes a breath and gurgles when she sees me. She stretches her fingers up over the edge of her box, releasing another giant wail. I lean down and scoop her up, hold her all baby-warm against me. "Shhh. It's okay."

She lets me soothe her, which is a giant relief. I'm good

for something, I guess. I walk her to the window, but she doesn't look out. Instead, she snuggles against me, flopping her tiny face against my neck.

I talk softly to her, put a gentle sway into my motions at the rhythm she likes. Betty's perfect for me, really, because she listens to everything without answering back, apart from a few small hoots. I'm grateful that Jolene has started leaving Nia with a neighborhood mama who watches several Panther kids. It's too much for me when they're both here; a toddler has to be watched at every single moment, plus Nia and I spend all of our time trying to figure out what the other is saying. Little Betty always understands me, somehow, whereas Nia simply does not.

When Betty's awake and calm, I give her a bottle, sitting in the tall-backed chair and holding her in the crook of my arms for safekeeping. Like a treasure. Her pretty, round baby face angles up at me and her mouth bubbles over with milk, and it's only a matter of time before my heart melts and I bend to kiss her forehead. Her little fingers clamp on my wrist. Jolene says it's good practice for when I have one of my own, but that won't be for quite a while, I'm sure. Jolene had Nia when she was nineteen, and that's a long way off for me, plus I don't even think I want to get married that fast. Mama was nineteen and married when she had Raheem, too, and look how that turned out. I get that things don't always go the way you plan, but I know how babies are made, and Sam and I never did that. I used to figure we would do it sometime, after we grew up, but it doesn't seem likely we ever will now.

Little Betty's feet drum my thigh. When it's just the two of us back here like this, it's so calm and quiet, almost a respite from everything. Sometimes I whisper her some of my secrets, because I know she'll never repeat them. I could hold Little Betty all day and all night and that would be okay with everyone, me included, but there's other things I want to do too. When the milk is gone, I coo at her for a while, then I set her up in her box with some toys to rattle and squeeze. "I'll come back in a minute," I tell her. "Don't cry." She studies me with large eyes, kicks her fat feet in the air. We've come to an understanding.

I pop back to Jolene's side. "She okay?" Jolene says. "Need me to go in there?"

"She's fine. I gave her a bottle."

"Thanks, Maxie."

"Sure, no problem. What can I do now?"

Jolene glances at her stack of numbers. "Well, I'm not finished here, but I promised to show you how to use the typewriter, right?"

"Yeah." I glance across the room at it, sitting on the desk Leroy uses. The sun through the big, clean windows glints off the silver keys. The heavy black metal body makes it seem so important. Everyone who sits behind it too. "I want to do that."

"Get out some paper and some ribbon." She waves her hand. "Envelopes and stuff. We have some thank-you letters to type."

Yes! I'm so excited. Letter writing is a big deal in the Panthers. Any kind of writing that has to be done is something important. For the newspaper. For donations. To let people know what's what and what we think about the issues.

Grinning, I bend toward the middle drawer, where the typing paper is stockpiled.

"Incoming!" Cherry's voice, out of nowhere. "Take cover!"

Hands in the file, I pause. Out the corner of my eye I catch sight of her body arcing in through the front door, a crazy leaping flight like in a cartoon.

The air shatters around me, a blistering pulse of breaking glass. The windows. I move to see, but not in time.

Jolene's hand cups the back of my head and together we tumble beneath the desk, her on top. The shots ring out over and over, echoing through everything.

"Three pigs on wheels!" shouts Hamlin. He takes cover behind a filing cabinet toward the front of the room. I can see him through the knee space of the desk, crouching like a cat, pumping a shotgun he must have ripped off the rack on the wall.

Lester lands hard on the floor beside us, rolls up on one knee, and starts shooting like it's nothing to him.

Jolene's breasts beneath the buttons on her shirt mash against my cheek, her free hand smoothes my hair even as she strains upward with her gun hand, firing through the open window. The way she covers me, I'm so small and so shut out. Terror and rage pulse through me. I struggle for breath, hoping it won't be my last. I want to fight, need to fight, but instead I'm helpless, frozen, unarmed.

I twist myself upward to see the storefront. Let it not be said that I cowered like a child when the moment came to be strong.

Cherry screams obscenities. "Pigs!"

My head rises beneath Jolene's. The windows are gone. Ragged shards at the corners are all that remain. The cop car rolls through the frame in slow motion. Bullets biting through the air like renegade teeth.

Hamlin pumps the shotgun. Fires. Pumps, fires. Pumps, fires.

Rocco lies flat on the ground beneath the windows, arm arced up and over, returning fire.

Cherry scrambles up from the place she landed in the

doorway. Arm extended with a pistol in hand, she leaps through the shattered window as the cop car clears my field of vision.

"Stay down!" Jolene screams at me.

But I've already seen everything. The red stain on Rocco's white shirt at the shoulder. Hamlin's gritted teeth. Lester crawling on his belly like he's back in the jungles of Nam, woken from sleep and thrust straight back into the worst kind of nightmare. Cherry, standing in the street firing after the cop car's taillights, spitting curses on the ranks of all the pigs in existence.

Everyone's arms, thrust forward. Armed and shooting. Everyone's except my own.

CHAPTER 39

THE FRESH SILENCE IS NOT SILENT. THE air rings with aftershocks. Little Betty screams from the back room. Glass crunches under Hamlin's boots as he rushes to check on Rocco's injury. Lester clicks fresh bullets into his weapon, standing sentry in the gaping mouth of the room. Gazing down the street, in case they come around again.

The moment it really does fall silent, everyone goes stock-still, heads turned.

The baby's no longer crying.

Jolene's strangled cry slices through me. She scrambles off of me, not painlessly, and trips her way through the rear door. Before she's even out of sight, Betty sets up a fresh howl, louder than ever and even more insistent. I breathe a sigh of something, but it isn't quite relief.

"Everyone all right?" Hamlin calls.

Suddenly I'm standing. "Fine," I say. Consensus echoes

around the room. The only one hit is Rocco. He holds one hand over the shoulder wound, waves the other like it's nothing.

"Not too bad," Hamlin agrees. "Looks like we can keep you out of the hospital."

Cherry comes out of the street and stands on the sidewalk surveying the damage. "Well, this is a righteous mess."

"No kidding." Hamlin gets up. The spray of glass from the windows covers nearly half the room. The air is dusty with chewed paper. The desks are dented, there are holes in the walls, the floor is littered with metal. Bullets, bullet shards, shell casings. Dozens of shots fired. It's chilling.

Jolene emerges from the back room, clutching the baby to her chest. Her fingers tremble against Betty's smooth bare leg. "We have to call Leroy," she says. "And we have to call a doctor."

"Much obliged," Rocco mutters, grimacing.

"I'll do it." I cross the room.

"The doctor's number's on the base of the phone," Hamlin says.

"Um." I'm staring at the phone now. There's a hole in the side of the phone base, and the cord has been partly severed. I lift the receiver. There's nothing.

By this time it's clear that the firefight is over. We're drawing a bit of a crowd. Clerks and shoppers poke their heads out from nearby stores. People have come out of their buildings to look at the damage.

Hamlin orders Cherry to leave her post by the windows and go next door to make the calls. Lester is unmoved from his position as sentry. He has his soldier face on, taut and uncompromising, like nothing exists but him and his gun and his enemy. I don't even know if he can hear us.

"Maxie, help Rocco," Jolene says.

"I'm okay," Rocco informs her.

"Fine. Then, Maxie, go ahead and get the camera from the back for when Leroy gets here." Jolene gives me the orders calmly.

I bring forward the camera and the broom and dustpan we keep in the storage closet.

"No," Jolene says. "Photos first. Maybe they'll want this for the newspaper."

Despite his claim of being fine, Rocco looks a little peaked. I set the camera on the desk and take a seat beside him on the couch, still holding the broom handle. Leaning it aside, I help him apply pressure to his shoulder wound.

"Thanks," he says, relaxing as I silently take over the bloody task. The piece of fabric feels soaked. I take up the cloth diaper that Jolene has laid on the arm of the sofa and discard the old dressing on the metal dustpan. The wound is bloody but neat. A little round hole, all black and red.

The bullet is lodged somewhere in there too. It didn't come out the back.

"Keep the pressure on," Rocco says. I push with one palm behind his shoulder blade while my opposite hand holds the cloth in place.

I know it's important, but I don't like sitting still, can barely do it. I want to start sweeping. Remove the glass shards, the spent bullets, wipe the whole place clean of what's happened.

"You okay, girl?" Rocco says.

"You're the one got shot."

Rocco shrugs. "A bullet is a bullet is a bullet," he says. "I been expecting this day for a while now. Least I ain't dead yet."

"Sure, but don't you want to aim a little higher than that?"

"Welcome to the revolution, girl." Rocco smiles sadly. "We ain't in it to survive."

CHAPTER 40

WALKING HOME ALONE, I'M FRIGHT-
ened. I flinch at every little sound, my
courage evaporated.

It's not in my head, entirely. Some-
thing about the very streets has changed. I feel the pavement through my shoes pushing back at me, fiery and
fierce. It sets me nearly running to get to someplace safe.

The apartment is empty, silent except for the strained
beating of the fan blades in the window, struggling to churn
a breeze out of the thick autumn air. I knock it aside, slam
the window shut. Drop to the floor beneath it, tug off my
shoes to let my feet breathe.

I lean against the wall, closing my eyes. I don't want
what's outside to come in. The air grows so still, the sweat
on my skin can't even cool. It dries to a thick muck in the
creases of my arms. I need to shower.

It's a long, slow path, me crawling to the bathroom.

It's a good thing I'm on my knees, in the end. I hiccup the remnants of my lunch into the toilet. The images flash like a slide show. Cherry flying into the room. The pulse of shattering glass. Blood pooling under Rocco's pressing palm, staining his sleeve. Jolene's desperate face as she dove atop me.

I don't understand it, really. I've seen worse things. I've seen Mama's face after one man struck her with the base of a bottle. Bucky Willis lying broken in the street. I've seen a shot-dead body two different times—once out the window and once on the way home from school. I've been pretty sure I can handle anything, all this time, after everything.

I reach into the bathtub, run the water cold. Strip. Roll into the damp pool, let it cool my skin of this ache. The soap bar is skinny. We're running low. It's one of those times when I just want the big, new bar, the way it feels in my hand, the abundance of lather and the knowledge that it'll be easy to get plenty clean. Today I have to work harder. The little bar slips and slides. I scrub for a long time. Everything is harder today.

CHAPTER 41

RAHEEM COMES BARRELING THROUGH THE front door. "Maxie," he calls. "Oh, there you are."

"Here I am." Standing in the kitchen, staring at the fridge.

He rushes up and hugs me, all worried and real. "Are you okay?"

"Sure." But the tears come out of nowhere. I close my eyes and wrap my arms around his middle. I let him cup my hair with a big hand and remind me that he loves me, without so many words. "Jesus, Maxie" is all he says. He holds me close.

Nothing can erase the memory, the slice of terror that slammed its way through me, sure as any bullet.

He draws back, finally. Brushes my hair off my forehead, smudges tears off my cheeks. Looks at me. I'm expecting words of comfort, though I can't imagine any.

"Let's eat," he says. "I'm starving. Have you eaten?"

I cock a brow at him, like "that's the best you can do?" He shrugs, and a moment later we are both laughing.

It's no surprise that Mama also flies home, worried. Nothing big that happens stays secret for long around here. "I knew I didn't like this," she says for about the fortieth time, pacing the living room rug.

I'm not really caring what she has to say about it. I've planted myself in the green armchair. Arms crossed, legs tucked in. Basically turning my limbs into as much of a wall as I can make them.

Wil is here too. Sprawled out on the couch, pants unbuckled like he owns the place. I've got my eye on him.

"I hear them chanting, you know," Mama says. "'Live for the people. Die for the people.'" She huffs her breath. "That's not for you, you know. That's for someone else."

It could have been me today. I stare at the rug beneath her feet. Stare at its burned edge. It is badly burned, recognizably burned. But in the year since it happened, I've never heard Mama take notice.

"The Panthers are doing their thing," Wil says. "I think it's cool, Maxie."

"This is my daughter," Mama says. "Stay out of it."

I want to laugh at that one. Stay out of what? Not our home, not our lives, not my every waking fear. Just this conversation. I would laugh, but my laugh place is stuck somewhere pretty deep at the moment.

I stare at the rug, at all the things she doesn't see. Doesn't understand.

"Raheem is eighteen now," she says. "If he's drafted . . ." Her voice trails off.

I glance up at her then. I'm scared of it too. The thought of him dead in some distant jungle, like our cousin, like the guys down the block. The thought of him even being over there, fighting. We've never been out of Chicago. I don't know what the rest of the world looks like, but in the newspaper pictures Vietnam seems like the strangest, most horrible place you can imagine.

But why doesn't Mama get it? Raheem is in the war already. Right this minute he's on duty, policing the police. The threat is real. The threat is here in front of us. I have the scent of fired gunpowder in my nose and in my lungs as ready proof.

Her foot catches on the rug's charred edge, but she doesn't glance down. Doesn't react, beyond knocking it back with her toe. An afterthought.

She doesn't see. Doesn't understand.

CHAPTER 42

EVERYONE HAS SOMETHING TO SAY ABOUT what happened. But it's what Rocco said that lingers with me. *"We ain't in it to survive."*

It sticks with me and it makes me jumpy under the skin. I can't make myself go to school the next day. Can't make myself stay in. I linger in the park in the morning, sit on the wall and eat an apple for lunch, walk the streets through the afternoon. Thinking about the bite of bricks on the backs of my thighs, the strange autumn sun, and the kinds of things like those that you tend to miss if you're dead.

Surviving the shooting gives me street cred. The guys tip their hats to me; it seems like they're for real. Not mocking. I think. It's not like I'm a hero or anything. Just, I've stood on the front line for a moment and lived to tell the tale, and that means something to people around here.

I know it's after-school time when the light is right and

I start to see kids coming, wearing their book bags and the regular look of boredom that it always takes a few minutes of freedom to shake.

Sam appears among them, rushing toward me with his arms up like "Where have you been?"

"Here you are," he says, stopping a foot away. Why is he stopping?

I cross my arms over my chest. "Here I am."

"I heard what happened. You okay?"

There was a time I would have wanted to run to him, tell him the yes and the no and everything in between. A time that hasn't quite passed.

"I'm okay."

He touches my arm, the way he used to. "Really?"

I hold it together, tell myself that Sam, too, has faced bullets. Only for him, it all ended a lot worse. No right to complain in the face of that.

"Sure."

"I'm glad you're okay." He shuffles his feet.

"Thanks, Sam," I say. "I guess I'll see you around."

"No," he says.

"What?"

"I want to see you. I don't want to guess."

My face turns warm. "I want to see you, too." But there are reasons . . .

Sam puts his arm around me, hugs me. I let my face rest on his shoulder for a moment before I pull away.

Are we together, or not? We don't talk about it. We linger near each other, walking, not talking, and there's solace in his presence. In our presence together.

C H A P T E R **4 3**

EMMALEE AND PATRICE JUMP OFF THE WALL when they see me crossing the park toward them.

"You weren't in school," Patrice says, stating the obvious.

"Are you okay?" Emmalee says. They hug me, both at the same time. Lots of limbs and awkwardness.

"Yeah." I'm prepared to tell them all of it, about the ache in my stomach and the trembling in my heart. The feeling like everything is broken, and what I know I have to do.

"Do you see now, why we can't go there?" Patrice blurts.

I shake loose of them. "I'm on my way there now." Anything else I was going to say stalls.

"Maxie, I'm really not sure —"

I slice in, cutting on top of Emmalee's voice of reason. "You don't have to go, but I'm going."

"We're not coming," Patrice says. "And you shouldn't either."

How can I explain? The shooting made me want it more, not less. It scared me down deep, but it also freed something there. Something I can't put back in place.

"The Panthers are everything," I say. "You know that. We all know that. We talked about it." A while ago, after Steve died. We sat together and cried, and swore we'd do whatever we could to stop it happening to anyone else we know.

"You could have *died*," Patrice says. "It's not fun anymore."

"Fun? It's not supposed to be fun." I feel my voice rising. My energy.

"We'll still come to the Freedom School with the rest of the kids," Emmalee says.

Patrice shakes her head. "I'm not allowed to ever do anything with the Panthers again. My dad said."

"Just don't tell him. Like before." But I can see in her face that blaming her dad is only an excuse. She doesn't want to come with me. Not anymore.

Emmalee takes our hands. We stand in a familiar little triangle. Nothing more has to be said. There are tears now. In my eyes. Patrice's. Emmalee's.

"Please, stay," Patrice cries, but I wish she'd said

nothing. Emmalee just looks at me, already knowing. Everything's different now. For the first time ever we can't find a way for it to be us three, together.

They're holding my hands, will hold them as long as I let them, but I can't say no to this call that is digging inside me. When the bullets flew I wanted to fight. I don't remember choosing; it just happened.

I pull my fingers free, step back. Look at the girls. My dear friends, my best friends. Without really knowing how it happened, I find myself walking away.

I don't want to stand alone. But as long as I'm with the Panthers, I'll never have to.

C H A P T E R 44

I KNOW WHAT I HAVE TO DO NOW. I GO DOWN TO the Panther office. The window holes are all boarded up with plywood sheets. Someone has started stacking sandbags near the door. They'll go up behind the new windows once they're in place, so that what happened yesterday won't ever happen again. Sandbag walls are already up in other Panther offices.

Jolene's at her desk working, like usual, with Little Betty bouncing on her lap. "Maxie? I didn't expect to see you today."

She shifts in place, scooping the baby closer with her arm. I have to tell her, before she hands off Betty to me.

"I want to be a member," I say. "A full Panther, with a gun and everything."

"You will," she says. Little Betty flaps her arms and coos.

"I don't want to wait. I want to fight."

"Honey —"

"Please?"

Jolene shakes her head. "You're so young, Maxie, and you're doing so well with the recruitment at school. And Raheem would have my hide, for another thing," she adds.

"You don't know what it felt like," I blurt. "They shot at us, and I couldn't do anything!"

Jolene looks at me, seriously this time.

"I'm part of this thing now. It's part of me, too." I lean on the desk, trying to make her understand. I know what it's about now. I know what you have to give up. "It's like Fred says: 'You can kill the revolutionary, but you can't kill the revolution.'"

"Honey, you don't just wake up one morning ready to die for the revolution."

"I'm ready."

"No. Maxie, no one wants that for you." She smiles, that grown-up way that makes me feel like such a kid. But I'm not anymore. I've seen the bullets. I know how it feels, know that I can handle it.

She touches my hand. "There's time. When you start your training—"

"I'm ready now."

"We have training for a reason."

"They came for us, and I hid under the table." Tears well up in my eyes.

Jolene throws her free arm around me. "Honey, we all did. We had to."

"Cherry was brave." The image of her leaping through the window, gun drawn and blasting as the last of the shots rang out, stuck in my brain. How she'd stood in the street screaming after the pigs.

Jolene breathes out a laugh. "Cherry's insane."

"Yeah."

"We all just want you safe, you know."

"Are any of us really safe?" I whisper.

Jolene slides her fingers through the hair at the side of my face, all motherly. I fight the urge to turn my cheek into her palm.

"You were so brave," she says. "I was right next to you. If you'd seen what I saw, you wouldn't doubt that you'll be a great Panther."

I don't doubt it. I want to prove it.

Jolene does it again. Smoothes back my hair, like a mother, which I know she is. "Beautiful girl," she says. "Your moment will come."

fireinthestreets

C H A P T E R 4 5

CAN'T SLEEP FOR THINKING. RAHEEM IS OUT, Mama's out. I have the place to myself and every corner is filling up with thoughts that will not quit. Thoughts about the past few days.

Emmalee and Patrice rushing up to me at The Breakfast, dragging me to sit with them, like usual. "We have to still be friends, you know." Patrice trips over the words like they can't come out fast enough. "You don't have to be at the Panther office all the time, do you?"

Me replying, "I guess not." Not wanting to lose them, not even a little bit. Feeling grateful.

Going to the Panther office. Jolene quietly handing me Little Betty. Stamping envelopes all afternoon. Maybe nothing about the world has changed at all. Only me.

I hear the keys jingling in the hallway, then the cursing. Jingling for a while longer before the door actually opens. I sit up on the couch.

Mama flops in the door, tripping against her dangling pocketbook. Shoes already off and in her hand. Not pretty.

It's not so common for Mama to come home drunk. Least not without a man to prop her up. Even then the times are few and far between.

"You're awake," she says. "Don't look at me."

"I'm not looking." I roll off the cushions and go to help her. I take the purse and the shoes and throw them by the door. Lead her to the bathroom, before she settles on the couch and passes out. We learned this one the hard way.

She leans on me until I get her out of her stockings and skirt. She's wearing the pretty panties, the black ones with the lace edge.

I sit on the side of the tub while she goes. She leans her forehead on the counter in a way that's probably going to leave a dent on her face.

"What happened, Mama?" I whisper.

"Don't you worry. I'm going to fix it. They can't keep me down. Not me."

I don't like the sound of that. She's crying a little now. I get her off the toilet and we start toward her bedroom.

"Where's Wil?" I say, suspecting.

The string of curses tells a story I don't need to know the details of.

I slide my arms around her. "Sorry, Mama." And I am.

He was one of the good ones, I was starting to think. Maybe not, for things to end up like this.

"There'll be someone else." I know it. I fear it. "Someone better," I whisper, hoping it hard.

She laughs into my neck. "You think you know the world, little girl."

"No, I don't know that much," I admit. "Everyone tells me I don't. Lay down, Mama."

She crawls into bed. I draw her covers up and sit on the side, like she sometimes does for me. "It's best when it's just us, anyway," I tell her. "It's going to be okay." I don't know if it is or not, but I want to pretend it is.

Her hand comes up, rubs my face. "You're a good girl. But starry eyes never got anyone out of no ghetto."

Then her head lolls against the pillow, her fingers fall lax over my shoulder and down my arm. She's out.

I kiss her cheek, push a clump of sweaty hair out of her eyes.

She doesn't know I see her like this. Her foggy morning head forgets and we never speak of it again.

It's how I get away with sliding under the sheets with her. Turning her on her side and tucking myself against her warmth. Molding her arms around me like I'm little again and nothing in the world can touch me.

CHAPTER 46

I WAKE IN MAMA'S BED, ALONE. THE DOOR IS closed, but I can hear them arguing beyond it. Raheem says something about being responsible; Mama says something about needing time. I leap out of the bed as the front door slams.

I burst out of the bedroom to find Raheem alone in the kitchen. He stands with his arms braced against the counter.

"Where's Mama?"

He straightens up. "She's not here."

"What do you mean, she's not here?" On a morning like this she ought to be lying on the sofa, still halfway sleeping it off.

"She just left." Pause. "Said she went to look for a job," Raheem adds in his lying voice.

My heartbeat slows. "A second job?"

Raheem looks away. "Maxie, I'm sorry—"

"She lost her job?" I drop into a chair at the table. "Again."

"Seems that way. Look, it's going to be okay." He sits across from me. Smiles as best he can to reassure me.

"Why were you lying before? Where did she go?"

Raheem makes a fist on the tabletop. "She has to find a job, so…"

"Where did she go?"

"I don't know," he admits.

Moment of panic. "Is she coming back?"

Raheem leans over and touches my hand. "It's not like that," he says. "She'll be back. I think probably she went to George's."

"Oh." George's Liquor Cabinet. "Did she take all the money? You didn't let her take all the money, did you?" I would have hidden our cash last night if I had known it was going to go like this.

"I didn't see this coming," he says. "I don't know how much she took. Just don't worry about it, okay?"

How do I not worry? I look at the cupboard doors, wishing we had done more shopping last week. I look at the front door, wondering how long before they pin up the yellow notice that means pay up or lose the apartment.

"Stop," Raheem says. "I'm going to take care of it. I'll take more hours. Get a second job if I have to."

"Me too," I say. "I can drop out. I'll get a job and—"

"Maxie, for God's sake." Raheem bangs his fist on the table. "Stop saying that."

"But—"

"We're gonna get by," Raheem says. "We always do." He runs a hand over the back of my head, tugging a section of hair on the way down. It's all he'll ever say or do to show he's worried too.

CHAPTER **47**

SNEAK DOUBLE PORTIONS AT THE BREAKFAST, eat every last bite. I'm shoveling it in like I'm doing construction. Bulldozer is what comes to mind, but I can't seem to stop it. The empty-pantry clock starts now. Started last night, except I didn't even know it. I have to save food at home, but load up on everything else while I can.

Sam watches me eat with a funny look on his face. "You okay?" he says.

"Sure, why?" I practically choke on my mouthful of eggs.

He rubs my back while I'm coughing. "Just wondering. You seem a little . . . on edge."

"I'm okay." I try to slow down, but it's like my body knows that hungry might be just around the corner. "Are you going to eat that?" He's left part of a biscuit on his plate.

"Uh." Pause. "You can have it."

"Thanks."

A short while later, we're walking up the steps to the school.

"Hey, Maxie. Do you want to come over for dinner tomorrow?" Sam says.

I've been to his house for dinner before, but not in a while. Not since we've been in our weird place of being together but not being together at the same time.

I peek at him out the corners of my eyes. Maybe he knows. Maybe he guesses. It doesn't matter. My stomach growls just thinking about it. "Sure."

I lie to Patrice and Emmalee so I can go straight home and be with Mama. I don't even feel that bad about the lie. I'm sure I'll confess later. Or maybe they already know, already saw through the veil of words to what is really going on. We have no secrets between us, in the end. Ever. But it's not yet time to speak of it outright.

Sam, I don't have to lie to. I just tell him my mom needs me at home, because for him that's a thing that will make sense without specific details. I'm sure he can't see the whole picture, because I've never been good at explaining things about home to him. It's so hard for him to imagine what life is like without a dad around. He knows I'm missing a piece, but he can't really recognize the shape of it.

"Mama?" I come inside and she's sitting at the table, hunched over the newspaper classifieds.

"I have to find a job, baby," she says, by which she means "leave me to it."

She is drinking from a very large malt liquor bottle. That's about the cheapest drink you can buy at George's, so I can tell that she's seriously worried.

"I can help." I sit down across the table. "Pass me a page."

"I'm doing it okay," Mama says, waving her thick red marker at me.

After a few minutes of letting it go, I ask, "What happened?"

"I'm going to fix it," she says, with no further explanation.

I'm curious, but not curious enough to press her with more questions. Sometimes she loses jobs because she messes something up, like showing up late too many days in a row, or making a bad mistake in front of somebody who matters. She lost an office job for lateness; they didn't care that the buses don't run on exact schedules, so it was kind of a gamble every day what time she would get there. She lost a retail job because she broke too many glasses and vases and things in the stockroom.

Other times, the places cut out jobs for no reason. She lost a maid job that way, and a couple of different factory jobs when they got new machines in that could do the work of people.

I sit with Mama as she circles ad after ad. There's always lots of possibilities, but only a few of them will ever pan out. We just never know which ones.

There's nothing much in the kitchen. Two cans of soup, some rice and beans. I crank open one soup and pour it into the saucepan. I add a few cans of water, more than you're supposed to, but just enough to stretch it between the three of us. "Keep it low," Mama says of the burner as I strike the match to light it. I already know. Everything is low. The lamps all unplugged and the overhead light switched off. Cupping the match, I swivel to the opposite counter and light the row of fat pillar candles Mama has laid out and waiting. They bring a soft glow to the room as dusk falls outside the window.

The power isn't shut off yet, but it was all we could do to pay last month's bill, and so we ought to start watching for this month. I carry one pillar to the table, where Mama is still bent over the paper. "Watch it doesn't boil," she says. The strain in her voice makes my heart beat faster, feeling the echo of times that were a lot worse than now.

"I know," I say. We lost most of a pot of soup that way once. In one of the worst times, when the yellow notice was up and the power was off and I went to the store with our last few cents and brought back the soup. While it was heating, the landlord came to the door and yelled at us about paying the rent. Raheem and I hid behind the couch, afraid, while Mama promised the man everything, anything, if we could just have a few more days. The door slammed shut, and she leaned against it, saying "Thank God" over and over, and that's when we first smelled the burning. Mama ran to the stove and yanked off the pot, but all the liquid had boiled off and the rest was suck to the bottom, turning black. Mama sat on the kitchen floor and cried. I hid behind the couch and cried, too.

Raheem knew what to do. He took the hot pan from her hand and filled it up again with water. He rubbed the bottom of the pan with a spoon until the burned stuff came off, and then he put it back on the burner until the water was warm. We ate it. It tasted charbroiled, but it was better than nothing. Though it turned us off soup for a while.

I go to the stove and watch the soup, stirring carefully until the little bubbles start to pop on its surface. "It's ready."

"Eat half and save the rest for your brother. I'm not hungry." She sips from the tall bottle.

C H A P T E R **4 8**

OING HOME WITH SAM IS FUN, BECAUSE it's like escaping to an entirely different world. He lives a whole walk away from the projects. He has a real house, sitting in a row with other houses that all look more or less the same. He has a driveway for his dad's car. We wander down his block. He holds my hand with the usual quietness about him. I wonder what is going to be for dinner. His mom is a good cook, so whatever it is, I'm looking forward to it.

Mrs. Childs greets me with a hug. She frames my face with her hands and says, "Let me look at you. It's been a while since we've seen you."

Sam takes off his jacket—Steve's jacket—and hangs it on a hook by the door. I'm a little surprised. I never thought of his wearing it as something he only does out in the world. I thought it was something he did because he couldn't help it.

"Your father's on his way," she says. "We'll be eating soon."

We go to his room for a little while. It seems bigger in here than it used to, for some reason, but I don't mention it because I assume it's the size of Steve's absence. You can feel it in the whole house. Then I remember that there used to be a big castle thing, made out of blocks, in the corner of their room that took up a bunch of space. There's no trace of it now.

"What happened to your . . . thing." I gesture with my hand.

"I took it down," he says.

We sit on the bed and look at a magazine he has with pictures of buildings in it. He likes to look at the pictures that show the outsides of the buildings, but I like to look at the way they're decorated on the inside. So we spend a while looking at every single page, except the ads. Usually when we sit this close, we end up kissing, but that would be weird here, in his room.

Then his mom calls, "Set the table, please," and we go ahead and do that. We take seats at the table.

Sam's mom comes out of the kitchen carrying a bowl of potato salad, sees me sitting there, and starts crying. Nothing else happens. She doesn't stop walking or try to dry the tears. The bowl clatters gently to the table and she arranges the serving spoon. Looks at me. The crying is louder now.

She goes to the sideboard and brings out an extra hot plate. Sets it on the table. Looks at me. Her face is a fast-flowing river. Her shoulders tremble.

I look to Sam, alarmed.

"It'll be over in a minute," he tells me. His mom nods. I think she's trying to smile. Maybe I shouldn't watch. I turn toward the photos on the wall.

Mrs. Childs is gasping, weeping. She clutches the back of a chair and lowers her head. I think I've made it worse. Tears spring up in my own eyes, seeing it all laid out before me. Family photos. Two good-looking boys, all different ages. Smiling.

Then it's done. She stops, breathes a shaky sigh, and retreats to the kitchen.

"I think she hates me," I whisper, even though I know it's not the reason why she cried. Still, it feels like I caused it.

"You're sitting in his place," Sam explains.

"Oh." I jump up, which makes no sense. Four chairs at the table; I'm going to have to sit in one. "Sorry."

"It's not because of you." He fingers the edge of the tablecloth. "She cries when the chair is empty, too."

"Is it terrible?" I blurt. My face goes hot. Some things you don't say out loud.

Sam says nothing. He knows me and my big mouth. That it's one of those things I mean and don't mean all at the same time. I reach over and still his fingers. Slide back into the chair because it has to happen sometime. I can't eat standing up.

Mrs. Childs clatters around the kitchen.

"Should I help her?" I whisper. I've crashed right into their private sorrow. The least I can do is make myself useful.

Sam squeezes my fingers back. "No, just let her be."

Sam's dad enters a moment later. After he hangs up his jacket, he comes and pats Sam on the shoulder.

"Hi, Maxie," he says.

Then he catches Mrs. Childs by the wrist as she's exiting the kitchen. Kisses her on the cheek. Surely he can tell it's tear-stained, but probably it's not news to him, either.

Mrs. Childs lays a plate of rolls beside her place setting.

There's so much food on the table, it makes my stomach ache.

In Sam's family they hold hands together to say grace instead of everyone folding their hands in their laps like at Patrice's.

Mr. Childs says a short prayer. He even says my name in it, thankful that I could join them. He and Mrs. Childs both squeeze my fingers before they let go.

Then everyone starts reaching for different plates of food. Whatever's closest.

After a moment Mrs. Childs nudges me with a look. "Maxie, go ahead and start the mashed potatoes."

It's a big bowl with a big spoon, but I'm afraid to take as much as I want. I look at Sam, but he's busy forking slices of pot roast onto his plate. There are ten slices. He takes two. I don't know how to divide up mashed potatoes so easy. I guess I'll try two spoonfuls and see how it goes.

Not well. The mound on my plate is huge. It's rude to put any back, though. I set the spoon in the bowl. Maybe no one will notice.

"Don't be shy," Mrs. Childs says. "There's plenty more in the kitchen."

I stop my eyes from widening by looking at my plate. Obediently I take another spoonful and hand the bowl off to her.

After that, item for item I match the pile of food Sam has, except he only took two green beans, and there are many more than ten. I shovel off a big forkful and wait to see if it's okay.

My mama didn't raise no charity case, after all.

CHAPTER 49

AFTER DINNER, MR. CHILDS SAYS, "SAM, homework time. You and Maxie clear the table and get to work."

We clear, and set up our books on the dining table. Sam's mom does the dishes and his dad sits at his desk doing whatever it is that famous lawyers do. From here it looks very official and like it requires a lot of paperwork and sighing. Sam and I press our toes together under the table while we work.

"I'll drive Maxie home," Mr. Childs says around eight o'clock. But Sam hasn't finished his English essay, so he has to stay behind instead of riding along with us.

Mr. Childs opens the car door for me. I slide across the bench, run my hands over the leather, not even ripped at the stitches at all. It's not so usual that I get to sit in the front of anything. He comes around and gets behind the wheel. And that's when I realize we're going to be in here together for a good ten minutes.

A big man. A famous man. It's dark, but I sit proud in the passenger seat, hoping some people will see. I try to think of him as Sam's dad, but I can only imagine his whole name: Roland Childs. Eating at the table with someone special doesn't take off the glow.

The car rides smooth. He drives smooth, hands coasting over the surface of the wheel on the turns. I can't help the places my mind goes, imagining what it would be like if Mr. Childs was my dad. Sam complains about him being stern, but to me he just seems steady. The kind of person who's always there. The kind of person who protects you and who knows how to do what's right. I feel safe, riding with him.

We get all the way to the end of the second block before my mouth kicks in.

"I saw you at the Panther office the other day. I work there, you know."

Mr. Childs looks at me. "I know. I saw you, too. You're a very efficient envelope sealer, I'd say. You got through that big stack in no time."

"I've had lots of practice." It's funny that he noticed me. He's a center-of-attention person, and I'm always in the background. I've watched him up onstage a lot of times, leading marches and protests all over the city. Raheem used to take me to the demonstrations. We made signs with markers and old cardboard we found on the street. This was all before the Panthers. Before it turned out that there was more we could do.

That's when I realize I'm still rambling. I don't even know what I've said. I clamp my mouth shut. For a second.

"How did you decide to be a lawyer?" The question pops out of nowhere.

"How?" He pauses. Smiles. "Well, I like to talk. I guess it seemed only natural."

I smile too. I like to talk.

"But the real answer, Maxie, is that I never liked being told I can't do something."

I look at him.

"It was hard to get into law school as a black man, and that just made me mad." He thumps the steering wheel with the heel of his hand. "I had to try a few times before I got in. The boys were young—" He clears his throat. "The boys were young by that point, and it was a big decision, whether to give it up and provide for them with some other job or go after what I really wanted."

He stops, and I can tell he's thinking back to those days. Maybe thinking, too, about those little boys, little Sam and little Steve, all diapered up and chubby-cheeked like Betty is right now. It kind of makes me want to giggle, but I don't because it also makes me sad.

"Why do you ask?"

I don't say anything in response. Strangely, I can't find a way to say it out loud.

"Are you thinking of becoming a lawyer? We need more good minds like yours in the mix."

I blush. Good minds like mine. "No. It's not for me."

"Maxie," he says. "Anything in the world can be for you if you want it badly enough. If you work hard for it."

I gaze out the window, at the shadowy streets. The closed storefronts. Parked cars all cold and quiet. Trash drifting in empty lots. Guys on the stoops who are always on the stoops, never going in, never moving on. Stuck in the same place day after day.

"Do you believe me?" Mr. Childs says. "I'm not saying it's all going to go perfectly. But that's what we're fighting for."

CHAPTER 50

I LIKE WHAT MR. CHILDS SAID ABOUT ME HAVING a good mind. I listen to him say it over and over in my memory. Offhand, easy. Like it might be true.

I want to believe that anything's possible. I scrub the countertop by the sink in the Panther office. My fingers are turning to raisins. First the mop water and now this.

The commotion out front catches my attention. Fingers dripping, I hurry to see what's going on.

Rocco, Slim, Gumbo, and Raheem are back from policing, coming through the door with their shotguns over their shoulders. Rocco and Slim are arguing. "I thought they was about to fire on us," Slim exclaims. "Why'd you step back like that?"

Rocco barks back, "I thought they was going to fire, too. Tried anything I could think of to tone it down."

"Had to tone it down," Gumbo says. "You did good, Rocco."

"No," Slim cries. "We shoulda let it go, let them get right up in it. We'd have taken out four or eight of them before they hit us."

Gumbo throws up his hands. "You got some kinda death wish, brother?"

"Whoa," Jolene says. "Back it up. Four or eight of them? What happened?"

"Bad day," Rocco says. He launches into the story. It turns out they had to stop twice to intervene when the cops were pushing on people.

"The second time, they turned on us when we got up in it," Slim says. "A whole pack of them came up out of nowhere, like they was waiting on us or something."

"We were this close to getting shot up," Gumbo says. "We kept our heads on, is all."

"They were just trying to scare us," Raheem says. One by one, he takes the shotguns from the other guys and hangs them back on the wall rack. The next shift of policers, including Cherry and Lester, has already rolled out to relieve them.

"No," Slim declares. "They were ready to jump us. One wrong move and we'd be goners."

"It wasn't that serious. We handled it." Raheem drops onto the couch. I start over there to sit by him, but he jumps up, putting space between us. I hate it when he does that, like I'm not good enough to be near him where people can see. I don't always want to be in his shadow anyway, but I also don't like the thought of him facing down a whole crew of pigs on a weekday afternoon. It makes me want to go and hug him, like he did for me after the shooting.

"I'm outta here," Slim says, sailing toward the door.

Jolene blocks him with her body. "None of you leaves here until you talk this all out with Leroy or Hamlin."

"I ain't staying," Slim says, but he doesn't move to pass her.

"I got work," Raheem says. "I can't wait for them to roll in."

"Then you'll talk it out right now. With me," she says. She shoves their shoulders one by one, steering them toward the back room.

"Maxie, hold down the office. Don't let anyone back here until we come out."

CHAPTER 51

SAVOR THOSE WORDS AS MUCH AS MR. CHILDS'S. *"Maxie, hold down the office."* It's the stuff of dreams, of course.

The guys grumble their way to the back room, but I can already tell that Jolene's right to make them sit down and work it out, like Patrice's mom does if she catches us girls fighting over something. It's ugly for a while, while the arguments are all out in the air, but later it's easy to swallow the whole mess with no aftertaste.

Jolene unprops the back room door and closes it firmly. I'm left standing alone in the Panther office. This has never happened before. I've been in here with a crowd, all the way down to one or two people, but never alone.

I'm not sure what to do with the sudden burst of power I feel. There are about a million things that come to mind. Dial the phone. Peck on the typewriter. Look in the file drawers. But none of those things are truly off-limits to me. The thing that wins is the most mysterious.

I glide toward the gun rack on the wall.

Who knows what holding down the office is supposed to look like? But right now it looks like me lifting a shotgun off the wall, just to see how it feels. Heavy. I'm very careful not to set it off, because I know that it is most likely loaded.

The gun feels huge. I don't know that they will ever let me be a policer, because I'm so small. Policers are supposed to be scary and tough. At least I can be tough. And maybe I'll grow.

I put the weapon back in its place on the wall. I don't know how long I'll be alone, and knowing the Panther office, not that long.

At home that night, I think about the feel of that shotgun. I'm lying on the bed staring at the ceiling when Raheem pounds into the room. He sees me, stops. Everything stops. His movement. My breath.

The look on his face, it stills me.

"Heem?" I roll to my feet.

There's a lot that passes between us unspoken. Something that comes from breathing the same air in our sleep for so long. I look at him and know something has wrecked him. It's not my place to try and touch that, though. I've tried before and come away aching. Nothing doing. I can't get to him in this place, where he's wounded. Not at first.

Only after he's started in on whatever he's going to do to make it worse.

Last time I saw this look on his face was the morning of Steve's funeral. I came from the bathroom and he was sitting there on the edge of his bed. Frozen like a statue, only trembling head to toe. This gun on his knee, balanced beneath his gently arcing fingers. Curtain open, like he was inviting me in, so I went over. Lay my hand on top of his to stop it from shaking. All I got for my trouble was a lot of yelling. He slid the gun into his belt and stormed out.

We had been to our share of funerals, but that one was different. Steve was a better person, a younger person, a closer person to us. And stolen in such an ugly way, it still makes me shudder at least once a day. To be shot by a pig like that for doing nothing, well, it's happened to Panthers before, just not anyone I know. No one who's touched my skin or called my name, or given me advice on how to be a good girl-friend. I say I'm not scared of what could happen, because no one else is, and Steve wasn't. But it's awful. Everything that happened to Steve and a lot that happened after. We're still caught in the after, at least Sam is, and Raheem.

I step toward him now, toward the untouchable space around him. Can't help it. Something draws me there. Raheem looks at me, an icy, trembling gaze. Don't come any closer.

"What?" I say, dropping it into a space not meant for words.

"Stay out of it," he snaps, retreating to his half and drawing the curtain. Bed springs creak. Then silence.

I go to the kitchen, stare into the icebox. It's not eating time, but I'm upset by what just happened. Something is going on with Raheem, but I shouldn't think about it. I want to run in and shake him. "Did something happen? What's going on?" I'd say.

I can count on one hand all the times I've seen Raheem's danger face. The first time was when our real dad left, and Mama had to stop Raheem from sitting up each night, waiting for him to come home. After that, it was over some nameless guy who came up in the house all drunk and wailing on Mama. There was a third time, after I burned the living room rug—at least, I tried to. And then it happened after Steve.

I know what happened the day of Steve's funeral. Sam told me later. The hard truth of it. Why he left the graveside service early, Raheem's hand on his shoulder and Steve's gun in his belt. That Raheem took him to kill the cop. In the end Sam couldn't go through with it; even his love for Steve, his grief, couldn't turn his blood that cold.

For a day or so after, we thought Raheem might have done it himself. He disappeared with the gun and didn't come home. But there was nothing in the news, and Raheem showed up in the small, dark morning hours. No blood on his hands, but broken. I was awake, of course. I didn't sleep for days after Steve died. Raheem stumbled in and dropped onto the edge of my bed. He let me put my arms around him and dropped his head low. I didn't know what to do with him for crying so we just sat there until it passed.

I always knew what the danger face meant before, where it came from. This time, I don't know. If it's Ma, or the shooting, or the close call from earlier, or some other thing altogether.

I close the fridge. Nothing much in there anyway, and the air is starting to chill me. I close the fridge, and as I do it I think about doors. Opening them, closing them, passing through them. My mind turns backward, spurs me to dash to the front door, tug it open.

Raheem tries to be clever, but he's not clever enough. My fingers go up and I pick at the scraps of clear tape on the wood. He tries to hide things from me, but I always figure them out.

I run back inside and peer into the cabinet under the sink, where we keep the trash. Beneath a banana peel, I find the evidence Raheem tried to destroy. Scraps of yellow paper, torn small, but not small enough to disappear. Thirty days before the landlord comes and kicks us to the curb.

CHAPTER 52

CHERRY LEANS AGAINST THE BROWN-papered windows. Smoke from her cigarette curls around her hips. She taps off some ash and raises it to her mouth.

"They put in fresh glass?" I say. The plywood sheets are stacked and leaning against the brick.

Cherry raises a shoulder. "I don't know what's the point. We're just going to sandbag it."

I touch it through the paper. It's like a wall to the touch, but now we know better. So thin, so fragile.

Sandbags or not, it seems obvious to me why the windows had to be replaced. We could have left up the plywood, I guess, but we have to show them we heal. We move on. Business continues as usual in spite of their best efforts to bring us down.

"Here comes Hamlin," Cherry says, stubbing out her cigarette on the bricks. She squeezes my upper arm. "Better get your muscles on, girl."

Hamlin's truck rolls up, weighed down in the back with a load of sandbags. He waves through the window at us.

Rocco, Slim, and Lester pop out of the office. Lester brings down the tailgate and says, "Line it up, ladies."

I end up between Rocco and Cherry in the bucket brigade. Slim takes a place on the other side of Cherry. Can't help but notice how he's watching her the whole time. When he cracks a joke, he laughs along louder if she laughs too.

Slim pinches Cherry at the waist, wearing a teasing smile.

She smacks his hand away. "Don't touch the merchandise. 'Less you want to lose a hand."

Slim grins. "Long as I got a handful of that sweetness when it goes."

Cherry bites back a smile. "Dumb as a rock, but willing to go down swinging," she says to me out the side of her mouth.

"Hey," Slim cries, acting all hurt. "I may be dumb but I ain't deaf."

Rocco laughs. "Give it up, man. She's never going to go for you."

Cherry looks at me with this secret woman-smile. I'm flattered to receive it, and surprised I know exactly what it means. She likes Slim, doesn't want him to know it yet. And I think about how, for all the times I've seen guys looking at her, I've never seen her really with anyone.

o   o   o

My arms ache from passing the sandbags. By the time we get inside, my limbs feel like mashed potatoes, and it's only making me hungry. Between Slim's jokes, Cherry's flirting, and Rocco's deep belly laugh, the time flew by, but now I can feel how hard we've been working.

I lean against the desk, staring at the sandbag wall we've built. From outside it was easy to make light of everything, to joke about the grunt work and to be grateful when it was done. Inside, it's a different story.

Lester's outside tearing down the brown paper; we don't need it anymore. Light comes in through the top third of the windows; the lower portion is completely obscured by sandbags. They're stacked like cozy little molded bricks. Lining our space with protection it never needed before. Turning it from an office into a bunker.

Looking at it, I feel all over again what has happened. I feel it as hard as I did the moment when the bullets were flying. I love it, hate it, want to run my fingers over it, want to tear it down. It's right, though. It matches. The space has been transformed.

"We're in the paper," Hamlin says. "Did you see?"

"No."

He cuts the twine off a bundle of the fresh issue, and I take one off the stack.

"Page three."

Flip it open. CHICAGO OFFICE ASSAULT. The picture is stark in black-and-white. The flatness is what strikes me most, and the stillness, because the memory in my mind is alive with depth and motion. The image they've chosen is of Rocco, his arm bandaged and bloody, stepping out of the wreckage of glass and spent bullets. He advances toward the camera, pistol held low in his hand, while at the other side Hamlin has his back turned, surveying the damage.

I'm not in the shot. Not sure where I was at the moment it was taken. In the back, or already on my way home. I lay the paper open, smoothing it onto the pockmarked desk.

"You see they got my good side," Hamlin jokes. He heads into the back room.

I tuck my finger into the groove of a bullet streak on the desktop. I'm strangely relieved to see that things can't just go back to business as usual. The office is scarred. It tells the story, as much as or more than the photograph.

Raheem comes through the door. I look up just in time to catch him walking in, as if I knew he was going to appear right then. His gaze flicks toward the sandbags, then to me.

It's one of those times when he pretends not to even know me. He rolls by me and hits up the rifle rack, slinging one over his shoulder. Starts talking to Rocco. They must be going out to police.

Cherry and Slim have been sitting on the sofa real close, talking. They get up and join Raheem and Rocco, gathering gear to go out on rounds. No one speaks. The only sounds are little clicks of things being loaded and organized. They file out the door one by one. "See you, Maxie," Rocco says.

"Bye." I want to go with them. Want to do my part to protect the community, like I couldn't do the day of the shooting.

Raheem meets my eye again, and I still don't like what I see there.

The door closes behind them and then it's just me and Hamlin, who says, "We're walled in now, but good."

CHAPTER 53

E MMALEE HAS THIS WISE WAY ABOUT HER sometimes. A sixth sense, maybe, like she knows exactly where she has to be at the moment that I need her. She comes down the block with her book bag over her shoulder while I'm leaning against the windows out in front of the office, wondering how long I'll have to stand here before another assault rolls through. She takes one good look at me and slips her arm around my waist. Nudges the side of my face with her forehead.

"Come on. Let's go somewhere else."

She has Eldridge Cleaver's *Soul on Ice* in her book bag. We sit on the ledge and she tries to read to me, but my mind is floating in all directions.

"Are you listening?"

"Hmm?"

She sighs. "Do you want to read some yourself?"

"No." I like listening better. I don't have to work so

hard and I can just let it all sink in. But she's right, today it's not sinking in.

Emmalee closes the book. "Okay. Well, do you want to say anything about anything?"

I tip my face to the sky. I actually am fine just sitting here, in the sun and the breeze, quiet but not alone.

"Okay, well, I have stuff to talk about, but I can let it wait if you want." She looks at me out the corner of her eye.

My gaze cuts to her out the corners of my own. I don't know how I missed it before. That certain smile playing at the edges of her mouth. I look at her full-on, and suddenly she's grinning.

"Jimmy?" I say.

"Jimmy!" She squeals like the little double Dutch girls. Leaps off the wall in a silly happy dance.

"What happened?"

She blurts it out all in a rush. My legs dangle from the ledge as I listen. About the first kiss and the second. She does the overview, then takes me through point by point, every glance, every finger brush, every word and what it meant.

I can't help but smile as it all becomes worth it, the days and days of collecting coins from the gutter just to have an excuse to go in there. I jump down and dance with her, fist in the air and swinging.

I was wrong about the silence. Talking is good. Distraction is good. It makes everything seem okay for a minute.

We push it as long as we can, staying out into the low dark before running home and going our separate ways.

I hear sounds through the door, but not soon enough to know better than to open it. The laughter and teasing voices stall as I barge in on the scene.

Mama's curled in the armchair, sitting across the lap of a man I've never seen before. They both look up at me, startled.

"Who's that?" he says.

"Who are *you*?" I fire back.

"Don't worry," Mama coos, patting his cheek.

I'm frozen in the doorway.

"Run along to your room, Maxie." Mama's words come out all slurred. "We're busy here."

I think about it. Stay and hide? Leave and hide? Go to Emmalee's?

"You ain't told me you got a kid," the man says.

"Well, she does," I snap. "She has two." I can't help myself.

"I ain't signing on to no family deal," he complains, coming to his feet. He looms large in the living room. As big as Rocco, maybe, or bigger.

Displaced onto the arm of the chair, Mama splays her

hand over the back of it to steady herself as she works on standing up. "No, no, no," she says. "They're grown."

The man looks me up and down, like he's checking to see exactly how grown. He's well dressed like an office man, but carries himself like a thug. Been in the room ten seconds and I can tell it.

"She's a kid."

"If you don't like it, you should leave," I say. "'Cause this is how it is."

"Run along, Maxie," Mama says, more urgently. She's holding herself up by the back of the chair. "Let us talk a minute here." She weaves her way around toward him. He lets her snake her arms around his neck and kiss his lips.

Over her shoulder he looks at me still standing there. He snorts. "She doesn't know how to mind you?"

That bristles me up. "I do what I want."

The man shoves Mama to the side, and she stumbles into the chair. "Come here, girl," he snarls. "I'll show you how to mind your mama."

He takes a step toward me and I'm terrified. Ready to run.

Mama rises smoothly, intercepts his movement with a hand on his arm. "She'll mind. Won't you?"

But I hesitate.

"Go," Mama says. I'm no match for this boulder of a human being, but then again, neither is Mama. And Panthers don't run from a fight. Panthers protect their homes at all cost.

She nudges the man with her hip. "Meet me in the bedroom, darling." Shrugging, he lurches toward her doorway.

Mama whirls around. "Get out of here," she hisses at me. "Can't you see he has money? Don't screw this up for me."

Standing on the street ten seconds later, I'm not even sure I remembered to close the door behind me.

CHAPTER 5 4

CAN'T GO HOME, IS THE THING. I CIRCLE THE blocks, thinking about what I'm going to do. Emmalee's, maybe. But instead of heading back, I turn aimless. Soon the Lemon Drop Lounge looms up across the street. Cherry's hangout, I remember her saying. I find myself drawn toward it. Cherry knows how to handle things. How to handle men. Cherry can help me.

I've never been inside, of course, but that doesn't stop me from slipping across the street. The metal door flops open easy when I pull. I slip inside to the music of the slightest hinge creak.

I don't know what I expected, but it isn't the relative quiet. People line the bar, sit at small tables in pairs and trios, and no one is talking in loud voices. Ella Fitzgerald sings out of a record player somewhere. I expected something fancier, not a dark tile floor and chipped wood paneling. The light is low, from sconces along the walls and above the bar. You can't really make out people's faces until you get within a certain distance.

I cross to the bar, trying to hold myself tall. Bartender looks down at me.

"You can't be in here." His beard and mustache cover his mouth. The voice sounds like it's coming from somewhere else.

"I'm not staying," I say. "I'm looking for Cherry."

He throws a dingy towel over his shoulder. "Gotta go, kid."

"It's important. Have you seen her?"

He pulls the towel off, wipes down the counter. Throws it back on. "It's not a good time," he says. "You should wait till the morning."

"But she's here?" I squint around, trying to catch sight of her.

Bartender sighs. "In the back." He points toward a thick red curtain hanging in a narrow doorway.

"Thanks."

I slip behind the curtain. The room is small and the light is even lower back here. Several of the wall sconces have burned out.

I hear the metallic clicking before I even see her. I recognize the sound of a handgun being cocked ready to fire.

"Cherry?" I turn toward the sound, to my left. Her silhouette blooms from the darkness. As my eyes adjust, I can make out her features. In the candle-like light I can see that her face is washed in tears. What shocks me more is the way she's holding the gun, trained on me.

"Oh, it's you." Cherry lowers the gun to the tabletop.

"Yeah." I've intruded on something. Something terrible. "What's happened?" I whisper. She's alone in the dark, and packing. "What's wrong?" I look over my shoulder, like whatever Cherry fears might be right on my heels.

The curtain settles, and so do the shadows it casts. "Things you can't understand," she says, voice low like the music in the background.

Cherry lifts a short glass to her lips and drains it. "What are you doing in here? It's not the right kind of place for a sweet girl like you."

"Looking for you."

"Well, you found me, girlie. Sure as the sun shines out your ass you did." She laughs, and the curtain stirs so more light pours in. Whiskey light flashes in her eyes, glowing bright beneath heavy, shadowed lids.

"You've been drinking?" I murmur. It's not against the rules to drink off duty, but it's never allowed to drink when you're packing a gun.

Cherry leans her forearms on the low table. "See, this is what I'm talking about. Go home and go to bed, little darlin'. That's where you belong." She reaches beneath the table and extracts a bottle, half empty. Liquor sloshes over the edges of the glass as she pours. The pungent scent assaults my nostrils, ugly and familiar.

"I'd offer you a belt, but . . ." Cherry snorts, waving the bottle at me, then thumping it back down beside her.

"I need your help."

"What do you want?" Her voice thrums low from her chest. For a second I'm drawn close to her in some woman way that makes me feel older, like a friend, a confidante. Which satisfies me down deep, because it's why I'd come.

"I wanted to talk to you—"

"But what is it you're looking for." Cherry sighs. "After the talking's done."

"I—"

"Don't tell it to me pretty," she says. "Tell it to me real."

So I tell her. Everything.

Cherry sips her drink till it's gone, listening. When I'm done she's pushed the glass away and lit a smoke.

"I want to be a real Panther, like you, not like a kid." Panthers can protect the neighborhood. Panthers can protect their homes.

She nods slightly. I wait for her to speak, but after a moment her head nods lower, like she's going to lie down and sleep.

"Cherry?" I put my hand on her wrist. Too personal.

She jerks away, awake. Two fingers bracing her cigarette, the other three stroking the gun. Her free hand, the one I had touched, comes back across at me. She touches my cheek, all gentle and sad.

"Child," she slurs, in a way that makes six years seem like everything. "Be careful what you wish for."

"I know what I'm asking," I insist. "I know it'll be hard, but I'm ready."

Cherry lifts her smoke to her mouth and draws deeply on it. She's smoking this one slow, and though it's more than half smoked, the whole tail of the ash hangs on, useless, but like it's waiting to serve another purpose.

When she lowers her hand, she looks at it like she's seeing it for the first time. She holds it out to me. "What is this?" she says. "What do you see?"

"A cigarette?"

Cherry shakes her head, her eyes drooping.

"Ash? Something burning?"

"No. Tell me what this is," she says softly, tracing her thumb beneath the thick line of burned ash still hanging. I don't understand the game.

"What?"

"What do you want it to be?" The glistening sweat on her skin flashes as she leans in toward me. "The truth? A promise? Love?"

My eyes catch the precarious tremble of the thin, burning stick between her unsteady fingers. A tiny breath lodges in my throat of its own accord.

Cherry grins. A flick of her wrist and the long ash falls to dust.

CHAPTER 55

I FEELS LIKE THE RIGHT THING TO DO AT THE time. "I'm going to keep this for you," I tell her, sliding the gun from under her fingers. Cherry isn't being fully herself, under the dazzle of drink and the seeming protection of a dark room. She says nothing, but tips the bottle to the glass again. She can't help me now, in this state.

The gun fits easy at the small of my back, beneath my jacket and trapped by the belt of my skirt. I don't even wave to the bartender as I scoot toward the door, feeling the weight of it on my back.

It felt like the right thing, moments ago, but as the door squeaks shut behind me and I'm facing the street, I realize I've only picked up a fresh burden. It's not going to get me out of anything.

It's not a long walk home, but it's long enough to set my mind churning newly. The gun changes everything. It's what everyone has been telling me. And it's what the Panthers are built on.

Get out of here. Don't screw this up. Mama's words, sharp like a knife blade, cut as sure. I want to cover myself, to hold in the wound, but it threatens to spill forth. What happens after that? What happens when every piece of me that's aching tries to get out to the light? Who would I become at that moment?

It's cold out. So cold that it doesn't make sense that my skin feels hot. It doesn't make sense how bad I want to lash out at something, when really nothing has changed. The man is at home, with Mama. I can go there, with Cherry's gun, but what happens after that? To be a Panther means doing it better, doing more than letting myself go to a place where right and wrong don't matter, where there is only rage and it rules everything with its heat.

I begin to lose myself in uncertainty. The knife wound stings sharp and the gun is right there, holstered and ready to be drawn into fire. But the fire that would spring from its lips is nothing, nothing compared to the fire that devours the streets or the one that lives under my skin.

CHAPTER 56

I DON'T KNOW HOW I'M GOING TO GO BACK HOME. But now it's much too late to knock at Emmalee's. I tell myself I'm a Panther now, and Panthers don't sleep on the street. Not when they can take matters into their own hands. The gun is tucked at the small of my back. It's no longer cold. It's warmed to me. I breathe a last deep draw of the fresh air, and slide into the building.

Panthers are expected to defend their homes. Raheem has a gun that he keeps in the drawer, but he carries it with him when he's out.

I open the door, no idea what I'll find. Scared I'll find myself pointing the gun at the man, trying to make him leave. Scared I won't be able to.

Mama's alone. She's sitting tucked tight on the sofa, staring down at the rug, like she can see it, like she knows. The door clicking shut makes her turn her head. "You can't do that to me," she says. "Run off like that."

"Is he gone?" I won't remind her how it happened. The things she said. Let her paint the memory any way she wants to.

"I don't want you walking around in the middle of the night. You hear me?" Her voice is low and strained.

"Is he gone?"

Mama nods. "I'm so sorry."

My mind is not yet at ease. I try to force myself to relax. Let the gun remain a part of me that doesn't have to be revealed.

"Come here, little girl," Mama whispers.

I drag myself down onto the sofa, curling against her with my head in her lap. She strokes back the short frizzes of hair along my temple and behind my ear. The weight that I carry seems to matter less and less.

"You're my beauty, you know that?"

I close my eyes, my body tucked tight. I curl into her words even harder. "Yes, Mama."

"Nothing bad that ever happened in the world was your fault. You got that?"

"Yes."

"It's just bad luck," she whispered. "My bad luck. I'm not meant to be happy. I just keep on trying anyway."

CHAPTER 57

I'S A SMALL ACHE, BUT ONE THAT KIND OF LIN-
gers. I can't forget what happened. In my catalog of
worst things, its rank is very low. But still.

I'm sitting on the wall, waiting for Emmalee and
Patrice. I start to hear the whistles from the guys at the corner
before I even see Cherry coming. She's wearing a knee-length
dress cut low and tight. Shades that hide half her face. Hair
all round and tall. A dainty purse. High heels, of course. She's
swinging. The basketball boys start to trip over themselves
turning to watch her do that walk across the playground.

There's all kinds of power, I guess. Raheem's kind,
Jolene's kind, Leroy's kind, Cherry's kind. I'm going to find
my kind. Make them see it. I just don't know how yet.

I hold my ground as she approaches. It's the high
ground, the place you want to be before a fight. Emmalee's
been reading to us out of *The Art of War*. Not like I'm at
war with Cherry, but she does have something I want, and

what's even better is, she probably thinks it's the other way around right now.

"Hey, Maxie." Cherry reaches me, braces one wrist against the wall near my hip, facing me. "I think you have something of mine."

I smile. "I guess I do."

"I'm going to need it back, okay?"

"Sure." But I sit without moving, without reaching for it.

Cherry shifts her hips, impatient. "So, where is it?"

"I'm not sure if I should tell you." I try to sound grown-up and aloof.

Cherry raises her shades and plants them in the front of her Afro. "Look, I appreciate it, okay?" She squeezes my arm. "I was in a bad place, and what I was doing was messed up."

"You all right now?"

Cherry smiles. "Never better."

There's an edge to it, though. Like there's an edge to everything these days.

"Okay."

"Thanks, kid. I owe you."

I grin. "Really? Will you do something for me? I need some help."

Cherry steps back and surveys me. "Sure. I know a lipstick color that'd be perfect for you."

"What?" I'd been gearing up to ask the real favor. Now I'm a little bit thrown. "Sorry, no, I didn't mean . . ."

She waves a hand. "Lots of people ask me. It's no big deal. I've seen you watching me. You're pretty enough as is, I think, but if you want to know more about makeup and clothes, I'll take you downtown."

Cherry thinks I'm pretty? "Really?"

"Sure." She reaches into her purse and takes out a cigarette. Lights it. The sunlight is so bright, I can barely see the tip glowing, but still I'm reminded of the shadow edge, the dark side of things.

"No." I fumble for what I was supposed to say. "I mean, that would be great, but . . ." I take a deep breath. "Please, could you tell Leroy and Jolene that I'd be a good Panther? They won't let me in, but I know I'm old enough. I already work at the office every day. I'm responsible and I follow the rules."

Cherry shakes her head. "What makes you think they'll listen to little old me?"

They'll listen. I know it. "You're smart. People pay attention to you."

She picks a fleck of tobacco off her tongue. Stares at me. "Hmm. Well, sure. Yeah. I'll say something."

I sigh, relieved. "Thanks."

"So, about the other thing. I really need it back," she

says. "Where'd you stash it? Is it at home? Let's go get it."

I reach into my bag. Extract the gun, rest it in my lap.

Gasping, Cherry lays her hand over mine, covering it as best she can. "Maxie, what are you doing?" She glances around to see who's watching. "You can't be running around with that."

The cigarette drops to the ground as Cherry fumbles to open her purse and slip the gun inside. I can see that I've scared her, the woman I thought was unshakable. She slides the purse back onto her arm, puts her back to the wall, and looks around, trying to seem casual as she toes the cigarette to dust. I can't help but track her gaze.

People *are* watching. Of course they are. It's Cherry. Someone who's used to being noticed. Me, it's starting to seem like I could wave a shotgun in the middle of the street and no one would notice. Least, no one who matters.

"Sorry, Cherry." I mean it.

She repositions her shades, slides her cool calmness back over her face. "Don't sweat it, sugar. You want to live on the edge? You got it."

Then she's walking away.

"Maybe the lipstick, too," I call after her. She raises a hand in a half wave as she fades back into the corridor of catcalls.

CHAPTER 58

RAHEEM FUSSES WITH BREAD FROM A plastic bag, cutting the presliced slices in half. He has a few slivers of chicken or turkey laid on out a plate already. I don't know where it all came from, but it's clearly scraps from somewhere.

"Dinner," he says, thumping the plate down in front of me. It's the smallest, flattest sandwich I've ever seen in my life. And that's saying something.

"That's it?" I snap.

"Watch it," Raheem barks back.

"Sorry." Being hungry makes me cranky. It's a perfectly decent sandwich.

Raheem grunts. "You don't know what I went through to get this much. You better appreciate it."

I grab up the sandwich. "I do appreciate it." I take small bites, hoping to make the feeling of eating last longer.

I don't know how long we can go on like this. It's been

a lean few months, but I haven't been afraid of starving to death until now. With The Breakfast each morning to take the edge off, it hasn't been so terrible this time around. Mama's still out of work, but Raheem just started working shifts at a second job bussing tables at an Italian restaurant down near the Loop.

Halfway through, I set the sandwich down. Eating slow enough sometimes fools my stomach. "I can still get a job," I remind him.

"Your job is to learn," Raheem says. "Go to school. Get your degrees. That's the most important thing."

I don't know about that. Looking at the sandwich, knowing it's not going to fill me. It's hard to think about the future when you're running on empty. But impossible not to, when I also know we're running out of time. Almost two weeks since the yellow notice. Soon the landlord will come knocking, and there's only so much magic we can work to stave him off.

I take another bite, swallow, and say, "The rent is past due." It's time to let him know I know.

Raheem studies me over his half of the sandwich. "No, it's not," he says. "We're okay."

My nostrils flare. It steams me, when he out-and-out lies. I drop my food onto the plate. "I saw the notice," I tell him. "You think you have secrets, but I always know."

Raheem looks at me for a long while. "Nothing gets by you, I should know by now."

"You should just *tell* me. It would save time."

"I get paid tomorrow," Raheem says finally. "We'll be okay after that."

"Is that the *truth*?"

He shifts. "You'll see. With my second job, and when Mama gets back to work, we might be able to save a little too," he adds. "So hopefully it won't be like this again."

That impresses me. We've never had any savings beyond whatever's in the coffee can at the moment. The idea is even harder to swallow than these bites of dry sandwich.

"I don't want to seem like I'm complaining," I say. "Food is food." That's a stretch, and we both know it. Tuna out of the can is nothing like a good thick hamburger. But I know better than to think about better food while I'm eating what I'm eating. I polish off the sandwich.

Raheem's expression softens. "You're not a complainer, Maxie. I know that."

"I would never complain about not finishing school, either." I try to sneak that in on the sly. I like what he said about savings. If I got a job too, we could *save* the money.

Nothing doing. "Damn it, Maxie, if you say that one more time—" Raheem threatens.

"You'll what?" I snap. "You don't have any say. I could do it tomorrow, and there'd be nothing you could do."

"You are *not dropping out*," he yells, leaning across the table toward me. "I've given up too much. Don't you dare even think about it."

"The Panthers need me," I lie. "I can work half-time and be in the office half-time, like you."

"Where is this coming from? Haven't I made myself clear?"

"I don't care anymore," I shout at him. I don't know where it's coming from. Maybe the corners of my empty stomach. Maybe from seeing the yellow notices. Or maybe it's the truth in my heart. We need the money.

"You better do what I tell you," he roars. "I know what's right."

"I want to matter," I blurt. "I want to help." Out of nowhere, I'm thinking about Steve. How he was out there, fighting for something. How he died for no reason at all. After the shooting, I know that I could die too. Any minute. I don't want it to happen before I do anything interesting.

Raheem goes quiet. A siren curls through the silence, first distant, then closer, then fading again. I wonder whose turn it is policing.

"You think you don't matter?" Raheem says.

I don't say anything, because it seems so obvious.

Everyone's been telling me, one way or another: "You're not ready, Maxie. What you have to give is not enough." And I've been believing them. All this time I've been waiting for someone to say okay. Maybe it's time I took matters into my own hands. That's what Panthers do.

"Maxie—"

"I'm doing it," I say.

"You are not," he replies.

"Am so."

"So help me, Maxie—" Raheem sputters, so mad it's coming out his ears. His face turns stormy like he wants to scold me, but really, what have I done except talk about what's true? It's an expression exactly like one our real dad used to make. A scary-perfect replica. It's been such a long time since I've seen that on anyone's face.

"Okay, so I won't get a job," I tell him. "Instead, I'm going to be a Panther. Full-time. I'm going to live in that office. I'm going to die in that office, until they let me into the lineup."

Raheem pushes back from the table. "No."

"We got shot at," I shout after him. "Everyone else gets to use that to change things, why can't I?"

CHAPTER **5 9**

I N THE MORNING, RAHEEM IS SITTING ON THE couch, sipping a Coke and waiting for me. He watches me cross to the kitchen, where I'm mesmerized by the sight of a fresh bag of rice and a bowl of apples. Despite being on my way to The Breakfast, I reach out and take one. Bite into it. It's not something we could save for too long anyway.

Raheem is still studying me when I turn away from the counter.

Around my mouthful, I murmur, "What?"

"You want it bad, huh?" he says.

I glide toward him, riding on the wave of concern he's casting my way. "What?"

"You heard me."

I shrug. I don't sit, because he is and right now I think maybe it's good to seem tall.

"Jolene told me how you tried to fight," he says. "She held you down so you wouldn't jump into the spray."

"It happened fast."

"Instinct is fast," Raheem says. "That means something, don't you think?"

I don't know what he's getting at. "Why is it weird? Everyone else shot back. I would have too."

"But you didn't have a gun."

"No." I narrow my eyes at him. *And whose fault is that . . . ?*

Raheem bumps a fist on his knee. "Well, let's do something about that."

It's a long drive out to the training center. The longest car ride I've ever been on in my life, and the farthest from home I've ever been, too, I'm pretty sure. Jolene says we're going to a farm beyond the outskirts of the city. She's driving up front, with Raheem riding shotgun and me in the backseat. I look out the window at the city scenery going by. Then the buildings get smaller and the trees get thicker and suddenly we're in the countryside. It looks like it looks on TV, only wider.

Soon we're out among farmlands. The fields are fallow now, but from underneath the snow poke brown, shaggy remnants of plants. We drive through a cornfield, a soybean field, another cornfield, and a pumpkin patch. I know because Jolene narrates the plants that will grow there as we go through different ones. I'm glad, because I was wondering, but I never would have asked.

When we get there, Jolene parks the car inside a rusty old red barn. She hops out of the car, and I move to follow suit. Raheem leans back and grabs my arm, stopping me.

"Before we do this, promise me you'll stay in school," he says quietly. "No matter what."

It's cruel of him to ask for such a promise at this moment, when everything I want most is right at my fingertips. Maybe he knows. Maybe it was his plan all along.

"I promise," I tell him.

"Okay, then."

CHAPTER 60

JOLENE PLACES THE HEAVY GUN IN MY hands and molds my fingers into place. Her hand over mine is cool and steady. My palm stings. Sweat and anticipation.

"You feel that?" she says.

"Sure." I try to shrug her hand away. I'm ready. I can do it.

She holds me firm. "Slow. One step at a time," she says. "It's not enough to learn to shoot. You're going to have to learn to fight."

"I already know how."

I learned to fight on the living room carpet, when one of Mama's boyfriends realized I had grown breasts. It only happened the one time, and I won, but I can't look at that rug without thinking about it.

"Raheem's going to stand behind you the first time. You have to feel the gun kick before you learn how to counter it."

I nod. My finger curls into place around the trigger. Raheem's hands land firmly on my upper back.

"He won't let you fall, okay?" Jolene says. I glance back at him, the grim set of his lips, the concentrated furrow above his nose. She didn't have to say it. I know. Raheem would never let me fall.

I tried to burn that rug once. Set a match to the edge of its fibers till it caught and watched it start to glow. The flames rose, lapping like it could lick itself clean. Maybe me along with it. Raheem caught me, put it out with a bunch of white powder from the kitchen. Baking soda, I guess.

"Are you ready?" he says now, just as I feel the fire rising around me.

"Yeah."

Raheem gives me this nod, and while there's no way he actually knows what I'm thinking, it's like he does know. The way he always knows.

"Lift, aim, shoot," he says. "It helps to think about something you really want to destroy."

I heft the gun to shoulder height and suddenly the reality ahead of me grows much bigger than any of the moments before. I've waited so long to be standing here.

The raw stuff that just spills out sometimes, can no longer be contained in the little box I call me. So when I stand there, feeling it, all heavy like the weight of the world balanced on my fingertips, there isn't a thing to be done but give it voice. Tiny explosions in my hand, one by one. Shooting. Shooting, till every bullet is dislodged and the trigger clicks, spent. My shoulders rock against Raheem's steady hands.

"Good," Jolene says. "That's good, Maxie."

CHAPTER 61

TELL NO ONE ABOUT MY FIRST TASTE OF PANTHER training. Not Sam. Not Emmalee or Patrice. I can tell by the way we did it that it's supposed to be kept private. A thing between Raheem and me. I can see it clearly now, and I know he thinks he won that round. I'm still in school and now I have to stay there. But it was something, shooting that gun. It still feels like a fresh start for me. I'm happy.

I don't even mind doing the envelopes today, at least until Hamlin comes in talking about how one of the suburban Panther satellite offices was raided last night.

"I don't understand it," Hamlin says. "Fred Hampton hasn't visited that office in six weeks. Minute he shows up, cops storm the place."

"They're tailing him," Leroy says.

"Yeah, we know that," Hamlin says. "But this raid wasn't spontaneous. They showed up all ready to bust in. In force."

"Like they knew he was coming," Leroy finishes.

Hamlin shrugs. "It follows."

Leroy sits thoughtfully, arms crossed, drumming his fingers on his elbow. "Then I guess we need to start taking measures."

"So you're saying . . ." Hamlin prompts.

"I'm saying, we've got to get more careful about our information."

"Like maybe there's a leak." Jolene sighs.

Hamlin nods in agreement. It's like he's been saying for months now. I've heard him. "And it seems like it has to be someone who knows all about our business," he adds. "Not many people are kept up on Fred's movements."

"They're not held secret, either, though," Jolene says. "Anyone can overhear a phone call, a conversation."

As one, they look over like they're just remembering that I'm there. I'm not even pretending not to listen anymore.

My face wrinkles into a scowl. "I don't talk to no pigs."

Leroy smiles. Jolene laughs. "Honey, no one is accusing you."

"I'm not worried about anyone close," Leroy says. "But there's a lot of new people up in here day after day. Coming and going."

"Well, we need to start telling a few people. Be vigilant."

I can do that, I think to myself. I can be vigilant. A germ of an idea starts sprouting in me. I see everything that happens around the office. I hear everything and listen to everyone. If there really is a traitor, I probably know him. There might be clues I know already. Suddenly my belly tightens with excitement. I want to find the traitor and bust him. That would be a sure ticket into the Panther ranks.

CHAPTER 62

RAHEEM THUMPS IN THE DOOR, CARRYING a flat plastic-wrapped box. The scent of tomatoes and garlic curls around my nose.

"I scored a send-back," Raheem says. I grin, because the timing of the treat could not be more perfect.

"Hmmnnn." Mama rolls over on the couch, planting her face in the cushion.

"Cool." It's all I can do not to run and grab it out of his hands. My stomach is so cramped. I uncurl my legs and slide toward the table. Set out plates, napkins, forks.

Raheem opens the box, and the smell is overwhelming. I lean my face into it. "Oh, yeah."

"Let's dig in," he says.

Mama's pretty well zonked on the couch. All the more pizza for us, I figure. We settle into it, and after a few minutes of no sound but us devouring slice after slice, Raheem extracts a small white bakery sack from his bag. He smiles proudly and pulls out a strawberry cupcake, which he lays in front of me.

"What's the occasion?" I say, smiling slyly.

Raheem grins. "I'm not a total doofus," he says. "I remember when it's your birthday."

"Happy birthday, Maxie." Raheem hands me a package wrapped in week-old Panther newspaper. It's large. I have to hold it with both hands and it flexes beneath its own weight.

"Wow." The package is bigger than my lap, drooping over my knees. I hold it there, trying to remember if I ever opened a present this size before.

"What are you waiting for?" Raheem nudges me. "Open it."

I tear into the paper, which is wrapped triple thick. My fingers brush buttery fabric and my heart rises. But I don't let it leap. Not yet. My excitement hangs suspended; I need to actually see it before I can believe in what I feel.

I shove the paper back, and sure enough, it's real. I pull it out and hold it up. A Panther leather jacket. One of my very own.

"Raheem," I gasp. The jacket is beautiful. It shines in

the lamplight. Three buttons. A hemline that'll fall to my hips. Horizontal pockets at the waist. Rounded-smooth lapels. Seam lines under the arms, around the waist, and down the middle of the back.

"Oh, Raheem." My eyes are dazzled by the coat, but I drag my gaze to him. He's smiling softly, watching me. "How long can I keep it?"

His face tightens. "It's yours."

"Really?" It's too hard to believe. "How?"

"The usual way."

All I can do is stare at him.

"I bought it for you, Maxie."

"We can't afford this," I whisper.

"My problem, not yours," Raheem says.

"I don't want to be a problem." I want the jacket desperately. But I don't want to be a burden.

"I didn't mean it like that."

I fold the coat on my lap. "Raheem —"

"I got it cheap, okay?" he admits. "Jesus, Maxie. Just take the gift. You gotta learn to be polite."

I can't help being curious. And I sure as heck can't help my big old mouth. "I'm sorry," I say. "I just can't believe it's really mine forever."

Raheem nods. He gets it.

I hug it to me one last time before I put it on. My

arms slide in and it fits like it was tailor-made for me. "Wow."

"Looks good on you," Raheem says.

I run to the bathroom mirror. I can barely believe my eyes.

CHAPTER **63**

I T'S SATURDAY, EARLY, BUT I CAN'T WAIT. I RACE down to Emmalee's apartment. Knock on the door. She opens it, looking sleepy. "What?" she says. And then she sees me.

"Holy cow, Maxie."

"For my birthday," I squeal. *I'm going to be a Panther! A real live full-on Panther! Well, I don't know if this means they'll let me start training, but at least I look the part.* "Can you believe it?"

"Not really," she says. "But it looks good. Let me try it on."

I shrug out of it and hand it over 'cause that's how we do. Nothing will stop it being mine, and mine forever. The jacket looks nice on her, but seeing her in it makes it so obvious that it's exactly right for me.

"Raheem has good taste," she says, handing it back. As if she knows I can barely stand to part with it for a moment.

"I'm going outside," I tell her. I have to be seen in the jacket. "Want to come?"

"Nah." She yawns. "It's too cold to be out."

I don't care about the weather. I slap on my purple mittens and run out to tell the next person on my list.

Sam comes out of the clinic and glances both ways before he starts like he's about to cross the street.

"Sam!" He flinches and turns toward me. I rush up to him. "Check it out."

"Hey," he says.

"I got it from Raheem and now we match!" I stretch up on my toes and kiss him. Sam's eyes cloud as I pull away, and I realize what I said may have sounded not so nice to him. I got a jacket from my brother, and so did he, but not the same way. It seems like no matter what happens, there's always going to be that difference between us. And no way of talking about it is ever going to sound exactly right.

But nothing can spoil my excitement today. "Where are you going?"

"I'm—uh—nowhere. I just wanted some fresh air, I guess." He turns back toward the clinic. "Do you want to come in?"

"I'm not sick," I say. "I want to walk around. And show them at the office," I admit.

"It's cold," he says. His jacket is unbuttoned. I guess he

really did just pop out for a minute. "I'm going back in. See you later?"

"Later," I reply, heading off down the block. Looking around as I go, I notice that not all the parked cars on the opposite side of the street are empty. In one of them—a plain gray sedan just a few spaces down from the clinic—a white man in a trench coat and hat is sitting in the driver's seat, staring my way. I look directly at him, not on purpose. He averts his eyes.

What is someone like him doing here, I wonder. Strange. I peek over my shoulder again as I walk away. He's not looking my way anymore; instead, he's watching the clinic.

CHAPTER 64

I N THE DROP-DEAD WINTER, NO ONE WANTS TO be outdoors. Not even me. I spend more and more time in the Panther office, and less and less time with the girls, who often go to one person's place or the other to hang out after school. I miss them. But I can see why they don't miss stamping envelopes and making phone calls.

I'm quite used to the phone at this point. It doesn't seem as special as it used to, although it's always fun to dial. Leroy hates talking on the phone, he informed me, and he was delighted to know that I enjoy it. Now I get to make as many calls as he lets me. Nothing too important for party business, but I do things like confirm deliveries and remind volunteers when they're supposed to show up for stuff.

He even had me call the newspapers and the TV news one time when there was a bunch of unusual cop activity in the neighborhood. Lots of cruisers rolling through. We were afraid something was going to go down. An hour later, a camera crew rolled up in a van and started filming, and wouldn't you know it, the cop cars started leaving the area, one by one. Leroy goes, "Log that trick in the books. We may need it again. Nice work, Maxie." I felt important, for a change, and it felt good.

Today, Sam is helping me stuff coins from the newspaper sales into the little paper rolls that Leroy can take to the bank and turn into paper money. We have separated them into piles of quarters, dimes, nickels, pennies. Now I am stacking the quarters and Sam is sliding the paper sheaths on. Below the desk, he occasionally toes me with his foot and vice versa. Above the desk, we are being very professional.

It's business as usual. Cherry's on a heated phone call with someone from the office across town. Leroy and Jolene are bent over the accounting books, running her adding machine, and figuring out how much cash we need to get through the month. Behind us, Hamlin and Lester are getting each other riled up over talk about Cold War politics and the plight of the worker in the global economy. I could follow the debate for a while, but now it's well over my head, plus I'm occupied with counting. Some neighborhood ladies in the back room are meeting about the upcoming clothing drive.

Things are quiet, until they aren't.

The door slams open. Gumbo runs breathless into the office. Everyone turns at once, pausing everything. It's that kind of entrance.

"Trouble," Gumbo pants. "Pigs got Rocco and Slim. We only just got away."

Coming in behind him, Raheem says something too, but it's drowned out by the explosion of questions and reactions to Gumbo's outburst.

My fingers tremble, spilling a stack of quarters. Rocco? Slim? A stab of ache strikes my stomach. When someone goes in, there's always a chance he won't come back out. What would things be like around here without Slim's constant joking and Rocco's laughter to lighten the mood?

My eyes cut to Cherry as she fumbles the phone back onto the cradle and rises to her feet, looking horrified.

"Simmer down," Leroy shouts over the din. "First off, are you guys all right?"

Gumbo nods. "Skin of our teeth, man."

Raheem looks shaken. He drops onto the couch and rests his head in his hands. He doesn't even stop me from coming to sit by him and putting my hand on his shoulder.

"What happened?" Hamlin asks, coming forward.

Raheem remains silent. Gumbo takes the lead. "Nothing, far as we can tell. We were meeting up to police. They were just standing by the car waiting for us, and boom."

Raheem lifts his head. "I was coming round the corner. Running a few minutes late. I saw it happen."

"I was half a block behind him," Gumbo says. "Jogged to catch up and I was all joking like if two of us is late, they can't get mad. They was cuffed and halfway in the car 'fore I got the whole sentence out."

"What was the charge?" Leroy says.

"We didn't ask," Raheem says. "We got the hell out of there."

"The way those pigs came up on them," Gumbo says, shaking his head. "It was a planned arrest. They didn't do anything. We thought they'd haul us in too."

"It's okay," Hamlin says. He lifts the phone from the desk beside Cherry. Dials. "We'll get our lawyers down there right now to deal with it."

"No kinda warning. They just took 'em down." Gumbo grits his teeth. "Shit, we shoulda been there on time. Maybe we coulda stopped it."

Raheem lowers his face into his hands again. I squeeze his shoulder, thinking, *No, then they might have gotten you, too.*

CHAPTER 6 5

LEROY GOES AND STANDS IN FRONT OF THE office door, with his back to it, like he's going to block people from entering. He surveys the faces in the room, nods, then orders Lester to close the back room door. "Leave the ladies to meet in peace," he says, but his voice is tight, and there's more going on.

All eyes are on him. "I need to understand exactly what's happening here," Leroy says. "And everyone in this room needs to hear why."

"Let's talk it through, point by point," Hamlin says. He knows where Leroy is going with this. Suddenly, so do I.

"Why didn't you meet up at the office before your shift?" Leroy says.

Gumbo shrugs. "Sometimes we leave from here, but sometimes we meet other places."

Leroy knows this already. "The reason for that is

unpredictability," he says. "If it was a planned arrest, I want to know how they knew where to find you."

"We're never that hard to find," Gumbo says slowly. "We follow the pigs."

"But you weren't following them yet," Hamlin interjects. "The guys weren't even in the car, you said."

"Exactly." Leroy begins to pace.

"It's riskier for them," Sam says. "Pulling people out of a car. Things go wrong." There's a moment of respectful silence, due to how well he knows how badly a cop stop can go wrong.

"And by then we're armed," Lester points out. "We could fight back. But if a couple of guys are standing around, waiting for their shift to start . . ."

"Okay," Leroy says. "Now the timing makes sense. So how did they know you would be there?"

Raheem's shoulder tenses under my fingers. "What are you saying?"

Leroy stops, looks out over all of us with that stage presence of his that sometimes comes out of nowhere. "We need to be more careful about how we share information. And we need to be vigilant about who's around us, and who might be watching and listening."

Tension in the room. Everyone seems frozen. Surprised. Upset. Leroy continues. "Everyone in this room, I would trust with my life. We have to trust each other with our lives. Every day. But the Panthers are gaining new members by the dozens, and we need to be vigilant.

"The pigs are working, finding ways to get close." Leroy sighs. "And there may be a traitor among us."

CHAPTER 66

I'S HARD TO GO ABOUT OUR BUSINESS AFTER that. Hamlin leaves to meet the lawyers at the police station and everyone tries to settle back into work, but there's a heaviness about the room. Cherry drags a cigarette out of her purse, lets the smoke cloud around her face to hide the fact that she's crying.

Raheem storms out in a huff of anxiety and I know better than to follow him. Let him breathe at his own pace. If he needs me, which he will never admit, he always knows where to find me. I'm grateful he wasn't caught today, but thinking that makes me feel guilty, especially because of Rocco. He acts like my big brother, too, in all those sweet, annoying, protective ways, and I love him a little bit for it. I hope he had his newspaper clipping with him, WHAT TO DO IF YOU'RE ARRESTED. I hope he has it memorized, too, in case they take it away.

"Come on, Maxie." Sam nudges me. He's waiting to fill another tube with quarters and here my mind is floating.

"Okay, sorry." I get back to work. But as I do I catch sight of Sam's leather jacket, which reminds me of my own new jacket, which makes me remember that I've seen something recently, something that made me curious. Something that would have made me think *Be vigilant* if I had known to think that at the time.

"No, wait," I tell Sam, sliding out from behind the desk. "Leroy," I call. "I have to tell you something. It might be important."

"Okay, Maxie. Come in back with me." He holds up his hands, showing me the ink he's got on them from changing the typewriter ribbon. I follow him to the kitchen sink.

"I saw something suspicious the other day. A white man sitting in a parked car, watching the clinic." I describe the man I saw. "He looked like a cop. Do you think he was watching us?"

"Maybe," Leroy says thoughtfully. "That's the kind of thing I'm starting to wonder about. Thanks for telling me."

I nod, glad to feel useful in the wake of feeling helpless over Slim and Rocco's situation.

"Actually, Maxie," Leroy says. "This is a good job for you. Keep your eyes out when you're around the neighborhood, okay? You can be my eyes on the street. No one's going to see a threat when they look at you. You might notice something that the rest of us would miss."

CHAPTER **67**

I TAKE LEROY'S TASK TO HEART. I WALK THE streets in the afternoons, keeping an eye out for trouble. It feels like real Panther work, policing the police in my own way. Except I don't like the part where he said no one's going to see me as a threat. Like I'm not tough, or like I won't be noticed. As usual.

I know he meant it to be nice, that he was trying to tell me I can do something no one else can, but it hurts my feelings anyway. Because I don't want to be the invisible worker girl anymore. I want to be in the lineup. I try to tell myself I'm a good undercover agent, but it doesn't ever soothe the feeling that I'll never, ever fit.

As it turns out, I do catch a pig monitoring the Panthers. He's a different man than the one I saw outside the clinic, but I see him twice, in his car. Once in the early morning, close to the schoolyard during the lineup. The second time, he's parked down the block from the office with a notebook, probably watching who comes and goes. I look right at him while he's talking into his dashboard radio. He doesn't try to hide it from me. I guess Leroy's right. No one thinks I matter enough to make a difference.

I continue around the block so I don't draw any attention to myself, just in case. I'll report the cop sighting to him when I get back to the office in a few minutes.

"Cherry." I wave, skipping toward her. "Be careful. There's a cop watching the office."

Cherry waves her hand. "I never met a pig I couldn't charm."

"But why would you want to?" I joke.

She laughs. "You're a funny kid." Her use of the word "kid" grates on me.

I stop walking, annoyed. "I want my lipstick lesson now," I declare. It's time to make a change. I want to look like a woman. I want to walk down the street and have everyone take notice and know I mean business and they'd better stay out of my way.

CHAPTER 68

CHERRY PICKS ME UP OUTSIDE MY BUILD-ing in her car. It's long and white and very clean-looking. It smells like cigarettes and perfume inside. It smells like Cherry. Perfect.

She drives me downtown and takes me to the department store she likes. We walk the aisles of the cosmetics section. Several of the clerks seem to know her.

I'm attracted to the heady floral scents at one counter in particular. The salesgirl has twin blond braids on either side of her head, which sway as she bends forward to show me the selection.

"You have to work your way up to perfume," Cherry tells me. But she lets me sniff the samples and she smiles as I pick my favorite. "That's a nice one. Try to remember the name for later." I don't see how I could forget. The salesgirl dabs my wrists with it, and the scent follows me. I feel like an elegant lady.

At the makeup counter, Cherry dabs samples on the back of my hand, until she narrows down the good shades. Then she rubs one on my lips.

"What do you think?"

I think it elevates me to some other place. I think it's perfect. "I like it," I say coolly, because reality has started to sink in.

Cherry rubs that one off and puts on another. "Oh, this is even better."

Yes, it is. My stomach starts churning. "I can't actually buy anything, you know." It hurts to admit it. It was an impulse, coming down here. I didn't really think about how I couldn't follow through.

Cherry reaches for her purse. "Pick your color. Like I said, I recommend one of these two, but it's up to you."

"I don't have any money."

"Well, I do. So pick."

"No, I couldn't." My hand strokes the edge of the counter-top mirror. The reflection there isn't me; it's only who I want to be. Untouchable. Unreal. And about to disappear.

Cherry sighs, picking up a tube of her favorite shade. "I always meant to thank you for not saying anything about that night."

"What happened?" I ask her. The color on my lips makes me bold. For a moment, I am the girl in the mirror. "You didn't seem . . . like yourself."

Cherry's body stills. Our eyes meet in the mirror. Maybe she only sees the unreal me, the grown-up me, because she doesn't push away the question like before. "There's this guy," she says. "He wants something from me that he can't have. Tries to take it sometimes."

"Is it because you look so pretty?"

"No." She slides her arm around my shoulders, hugging me against her. "It's because he doesn't know how to treat people nice. Don't be afraid of looking pretty."

We look at each other in the mirror, two pretty girls, one real. Then Cherry releases me. "It's a small token. One lipstick, and I'll throw in one mascara. With your complexion that's all you really need anyway."

"Wow," I say. "Thanks." I should be torn, but I'm not. I want it, and Cherry wants to give it. Mama says we don't take charity, but then Raheem tells me I got to learn to accept a gift. I like Raheem's logic. It's more polite.

Cherry shows me with the sample how to roll mascara onto my lashes without making too many clumps. I'm not sure I've got the hang of it, but she says it'll come with practice. A cashier rings us up.

"This is really neat," I tell her. "Thanks."

The clerk puts the items in a little brown bag with a stiff

handle. It all seems so expensive and I stretch myself tall because Cherry thinks I'm worth it.

We go back onto the street, and I feel like a pretty person. A person people might notice. I know I'm no match for Cherry's looks and Cherry's body, but I suppose I'm one step closer.

"This is a good shop," she says, stopping halfway down the block. "I'm going in for some smokes, but you have to wait here. They won't let in someone your age."

So what else is new? "Can I sit in the park?" There's a little green across the street. It looks like a nice spot to wait, to watch things.

"Sure. I'll be along in a few minutes."

I'm standing on the corner waiting for the light to change when I notice a familiar face a little ways down the block. What in the world is Sam Childs doing all the way downtown?

C H A P T E R 6 9

SAM'S TALKING TO A WHITE MAN IN A SUIT. I start to go toward him, but I stop short.

It's the man from the car, the one I saw parked in front of the clinic. I have to do a double take to be sure, but it's him. The guy I reported to Leroy as probably a spy for the pigs. Why is he talking to Sam?

The man gives Sam a thick yellow envelope. They shake hands. Sam tucks the envelope in his jacket and glances around. I duck behind the building. I don't think he saw me. Then again, why shouldn't he see me? I don't have anything to hide. So I pop into view again. The man in the suit is out of sight, but Sam's coming toward me.

When he sees me, he freezes, caught in the act of something. "What are you doing here?"

"Who was that?"

Sam shuffles his feet. "Doesn't matter."

"Yeah, it does."

He starts walking again. "Look, I can't tell you that, okay?"

"Why not?"

"I just can't."

"Why not?" I'm scared now, because there has to be an explanation. There has to be something other than the only thing in my mind. Sam wouldn't. Sam couldn't. But my mind burns with what I saw.

He's annoyed, crossing his arms over his chest. "Did you follow me or something? Nobody was supposed to see us."

I'm thinking of Slim and Rocco. Little pieces of information floating in the air. Landing where the pigs can pick them up.

"Sam."

"Stop asking me," he says. "It's a Panther business thing."

Heat rises in my stomach. "What's that supposed to mean?" I'm a Panther too. It's one thing for Jolene and Leroy to look at me different, but Sam, Sam's supposed to be on my side. There aren't supposed to be secrets between us. "I tell you everything."

He kind of laughs. "No, you don't."

"Why won't you tell me?" The thought keeps sinking in, terrible and deep. There's only one picture to be painted here. Sam with a cop. Sam with a cop and an envelope. Sam with a cop and an envelope, Sam knowing all that he knows.

"Maxie—"

Sam, the traitor.

"I saw him before," I blurt. "Spying on us. I know he's a cop."

Sam spins toward me. "What?"

I dive at his chest, trying to get at his pocket. My vision is suddenly blurred by tears. "What's in the envelope? Money? Did he pay you off?" My fingers brush the corner of it, thick and full and smooth.

Sam catches my wrists, trying to stop me from pawing at him. I'm crying out loud now, locked in place in front of him. My hands are spread flat over his heart. His good, kind heart. I want to take it back, every bad thought. Every word I've spoken without thinking. How can it be true?

"I can't believe you would even say that to me," he whispers. His eyes, too, fill with tears.

"Rocco and Slim are in jail," I cry. "Don't you care about that?" I'm on a roll and I can't stop myself, even though I'm wrong. I have to be wrong. But I felt the edges of the bills, crisp and neat, through the gap in the flap of the envelope. My fingertip is bleeding, sliced in tiny parallel lines.

Sam just stares at me. "My brother *died*. How could you

think that I would ever—" He releases me and steps back.

I shake my head. Shaking all over, really. "I don't know," I say. "So just tell me the truth. Why are you here?"

Sam buttons his jacket carefully, one by one, sealing his secret inside. "You don't trust me at all," he says. "Why should I trust you?"

CHAPTER 70

SAM HURRIES AWAY, LEAVING IT ALL UNFIN-
ished. Leaving all the wrong things said and
unsaid. I stumble toward the park, collapse on
a bench. My shoulders shake with sobs. There
has to be a reason—a good reason, a normal reason—why
Sam is taking money from a white cop in a secret meeting.
He can't be the traitor, I know it in my gut, but my mind
keeps going back there and I can't get my thoughts off
this train.

Cherry finds me, finds my little shopping bag all loose
and strewn about me. She sits down beside me. "I wasn't
gone that long," she says. "What happened?"

My response is to start sobbing louder. I can't bring
myself to say the truth out loud. Cherry slides her arm
around me. "I've never seen anyone this upset to stop shopping," she quips. I shake my head. I need her to know I'm
not an idiot.

Sighing, she reaches into her purse and pulls out a lacy handkerchief. I dry the tears off my cheeks and gradually gasp myself calm.

"You want to talk about it?" Cherry says.

"No." I jump to my feet. "Let's go."

It's terrible, what I've done. To accuse Sam of something so awful. After Steve died at the hands of the pigs, of course Sam would never . . . but he didn't give me any explanation. My mind works, trying to fashion one.

Sam lost the money and the man returned it. But why would Sam have that kind of cash in the first place? Even if it was all one dollar bills, it was too thick to be his allowance. And those bills felt crisp and new.

Sam placed a bet and the man is paying him his winnings. But Sam wouldn't know a bookie from a cookie, and anyway no one I know would lay a bet with somebody white.

The man works with Sam's father. The money belongs to him. I can almost sink my teeth into that one.

It wasn't money in the envelope at all, it only felt like it. It was . . . papers cut to the size of money. Tickets? Receipts? Something important and rare that the Panthers might need. Nothing comes to mind.

I can't sleep for worrying about it. I don't know what

to do. I'm Leroy's eyes and ears. I'm supposed to tell him when things happen. Do I share my suspicions, even though I'm sure they can't be true? What if Sam can't explain, and he did do something he shouldn't? How would I feel if I turned him in?

CHAPTER 71

'M RUNNING ON PRACTICALLY NO SLEEP. IT UPSETS me still, thinking Sam might be the informant. None of my alternate scenarios make any real sense.

Before I tell Leroy, though, I want to confront Sam again, and see if his story changes. I'm walking it off, trying to get out from under the pressure I feel. Taking turns around the blocks and hoping the fresh, chill air will clear my mind.

I catch sight of Raheem walking quickly down a side street. He's almost a block away, but I know his walk like anything.

Spontaneously I turn in the direction he's going. Raheem can help me. I don't know why I didn't think of it sooner. Except he wasn't home last night until after I was pretending to sleep. This morning he was out the door before I'd wiped the sleep dust from my eyes.

But the answer is so obvious now. I can trust Raheem

with what happened. I'll run it by him before I do anything else. Ask him if he thinks it's even possible, what I'm thinking of Sam. And if I should tell Leroy just in case, or keep Sam's secret, whatever it might be.

"Heem!" I call. He doesn't hear me. Seems to be in a hurry.

"Heem!" I can't imagine where he's going, actually, because this road dead-ends beneath the highway and there's nothing but alleys to turn off into.

I follow. "Heem!" But he's already around the corner. I dash after him, but I come up short. What I see does not compute.

Raheem stalks toward a parked car on the deserted street. It's a clean gray sedan with city plates. A cop car, unmarked. A cop car I've seen twice before, staking out the Panthers. Today he's parked out of the way of everything, but that falls beside the point as Raheem opens the passenger door and gets inside.

I blink. He *gets inside*. With the cop. If it was anyone else, anyone who didn't know me, I would walk right by that car. My undercover moves.

But it's Raheem, and so I stand frozen. No idea how to proceed.

Moving along to the building edge of the sidewalk, I inch closer. I need to see it up close, need to know for sure.

They are talking. Silhouettes facing each other for five, maybe ten, minutes. It seems like an eternity, but anything would under the circumstances.

There can be no mistaking it. Plain as day, in front of my eyes, Raheem is ruining everything.

C H A P T E R 7 2

THE CAR DOOR OPENS. INSTINCT TELLS me to hide, but I can't get my feet to move. Raheem comes down the alley. Stops short when he catches sight of me.

"Maxie," he says. My name falls heavy on the pavement between us. "You followed me?"

The words are tripped up on my tongue. A thing that never happens to me. Raheem seems not sure what to say either. "You followed me?" he repeats.

It all came so easy yesterday. I spit so many words at Sam, words I can never take back. Here and now, I'm bereft.

"I can explain this," Raheem says.

I cross my arms. "Go ahead." I'm giving him the chance I didn't give Sam. Not jumping to conclusions. I was wrong about Sam. I could be wrong about this, too, I tell myself, but it isn't convincing, even in my head.

Sam is a person who came into my life, a person I've

spent an on-and-off year getting to know. He's new to me. Even when I kiss him, it's like we're still meeting sometimes. With Raheem, it's different. Raheem is a part of me. That thing we have, that unspoken thing, is stronger than either of us and it makes me know for certain things I'd rather not.

"We needed the money," he says.

I back away from him, shaking my head.

He reaches out his hand. "They knew, and they told me . . . Maxie, you have no idea how much we needed it."

No. Nonononononononono. I turn my back and flee. As far and as fast as I can. All the while knowing, I'll never outrun what has happened.

The world implodes around me. I run through the streets, aimless, no clue what I'm thinking, where I will end up. But I can't escape the sight; it lingers like a photograph. Can't escape the knowledge of what Raheem has done. I run to the edge of the lake, dip my toes in the icy water. Anything to cool the fire beneath my feet.

This is where we come. Sam and me. Sam, who I love, who I believed the worst of. My betrayal of him stings my skin. The world splits wide open in front of me, my every mistake roiling in the waves. A thousand grains of sand. Water lapping languidly. Streaks of clouds like claw marks across the ruined sky.

I let it out, finally. The scream bends me double.

A seagull caws at me, frightened. His toes skim the lake surface as he glides away to a fresh perch somewhere beyond the edges of my gaze.

For the first time I can ever remember, I don't want tomorrow to come.

CHAPTER 73

RAHEEM'S WAITING FOR ME WHEN I GET home. Sitting on the couch with his hands folded in front of him, elbows on his knees.

"Don't you have to *work*," I say, pressing the door shut behind me. Now that I've caught him taking a bribe, his real jobs are going to matter more than ever.

Raheem simply stares at me. It hits like a hammer over my head. How stupid I've been all along. How did I believe he could work all these extra shifts and still be able to do the policing? To still come home every night more or less at the usual time?

Now all the shreds of pretense are dropped. He doesn't have to work tonight.

"How much?" I ask.

"What?"

"How much money did they pay you?" I fight to keep my voice even.

Raheem rubs his hands together. "You don't want to know more than you already do." He comes off the couch, moving toward me. "I need you to forget what you saw, Maxie. I need it to be like this never happened."

Forget? "Did you think this was going to be okay with me?"

"We're blood," he says.

"We're all blood," I cry. "Skin. Hair. How could you?"

"You wanna sleep on the street? Someone has to pay for our life."

"Such as it is," I blurt.

Raheem's eyes narrow. "You think you can do better?"

I'm angry. Shaking. Frightened. "I don't know. Maybe."

He shakes his head. "You think this was easy? Jesus, Maxie. Why do you think I did it?"

"Don't—"

"I did it for you."

"Don't say that."

"We had no money," he says. "None. This Fed, he knew all about it, and they covered our bills. And then some."

"Why didn't you tell me?" I whisper. "I would have told you no, it wasn't worth it."

"We're okay now, don't you get it? Doesn't that matter to you at all?"

My stomach aches. "Raheem."

"Don't look at me like that. I did this for you," he says. "I gave up *everything* for you!"

"You *took* everything from me," I cry. "How am I supposed to go in there and face everyone now?"

"Just like I do," he says. "Do your work and keep your head down. Never tell anyone. I mean *anyone*. Not even Sam, not even Emmalee, you hear me?"

"So it's over now, right? You're going to stop?"

"Maxie—"

"What are you going to say to Leroy?"

Raheem grabs me by the arms. It's rough. A kind of pain I've never known. For someone I love to hurt me. I've been so careful not to love, not to be hurt anymore. The ache bubbles inside me, boils into rage.

"Let me go!" I struggle against his hands.

"You can't tell anyone," he insists. "Ever. You know that, right?"

I want to spit at him. I gather a pool in my mouth and pucker.

"If you tell, they will kill me. Leroy himself would shoot me dead."

I swallow hard, stop fighting him.

"You understand?" he says. "They'll kill me."

"I'll kill you myself," I hiss. Each trembling breath a coffin nail. Mine. His. I can't even tell. Maybe that's the thing with the blood bond. You all rise high or else all fall down together.

I've been living off the pigs. The truth consumes me, hot as the licking flames of hell. I tear through the house, to my room. I tear down everything, not just what is new. The pretty blue dress. My white sandals. I don't know when it started. When he first sold out and sold us to the enemy. Everything is tainted.

My beautiful, beloved Panther leather jacket. I strip it from my skin like it's on fire.

CHAPTER 74

THERE IS NOTHING, NOTHING THAT TOUCHES me anymore. The invisible thing that I have been seems fitting now. I don't want to be seen, for once. Keep the phone in my hand at all times so people will know I'm busy and not bother to ask me anything.

I see the effects of Raheem's betrayal everywhere. The legal aid lawyers come by, gearing up for Slim and Rocco's defense. They've not been let out of jail. The court is not letting us bail them out, for reasons no one seems to understand.

I miss Rocco's presence in the office. We thought they would be home by now, able to go about their business, just with a court date hanging over their heads. Cherry's eyes are puffy behind her shades, and even though she won't admit it, I know it's because she misses Slim.

She says only one thing to me about any of it. I come up

to her in the office to show her I'm wearing the lipstick she got me. I feel so pretty and grown-up in spite of everything. She tips my chin up with her finger, looks at me, and says, "Yes. It suits you."

I lean in and hug her. "Cherry." It feels right because I know that she has lost something, and I know that I have too.

She wraps her arms around me and whispers, "Maxie, sugar, don't put off anything you want. Not a thing. Not even for a minute. Just go get it, because you don't know when it's going to be gone."

And that's the end of it. I wish it was that easy for me, knowing what I want. To top it off, I'm all alone in this. Raheem told me not to tell Sam, not to tell Emmalee. When he said it, I was so sure I would break that directive the second I walked away. But now I realize how true it is. I can't confide in anyone.

Sam strides across the office like he knows. Knows everything. I have to turn away.

"Maxie," he says, and I put up my hand like "don't even start."

He can't know. No one can. I hold secrets well. It's something I'm good at. I run my mouth, sure, but not about what's real.

"Not here." The envelopes blur beneath my gaze. "Later."

I'm going to have to tell him. Apologize. Admit defeat and helplessness and everything horrible. He'll hate me.

They'll all hate me. For holding the secret. For not telling sooner. For being his sister.

"Let's go outside," Sam says. His eyes are reading me. Worried. Caring. I ache inside. Heart. Stomach. Way down low in the belly.

The window beckons. White light pouring in through the space around the curtains. I want to walk out with him. We've always been that way, needing space around us. Inside, breathing close, everything presses on us and we can't get out from under.

I want to take the hand he holds out to me, but . . . what happens a moment later? I'll speak the things I can't take back and everything will be over. No one wants anything to do with a traitor.

Around the room, everyone's working different tasks. Jolene and her adding machine. Leroy by the bookcase, surely thinking up words to use later. Hamlin reads aloud from a magazine, something that causes the people closest to him to be all smiles. Cherry tosses her hair and laughs, throaty and rich. Others join in, a happy chorus.

Sam turns toward them too. Toward the brief flash of joy lighting up the air. It's not a thing you can look away from so easy.

Shining, intense laughter, the kind that tastes like it's everything. Moment to moment, it all matters. After Steve. After the office assault. After Slim and Rocco, and all the cats behind bars. It could be over in an instant. The bullet hits and we all meet whatever god or devil's waiting, and knowing me, I say something stupid and end up damned for eternity in a sloppy hellhole. Worse than the gutter. So low.

I blink back everything. Panthers don't cry.

Boots on the floor. Eyes forward.

"I have work to do."

CHAPTER 75

SAM DOESN'T LET IT GO. WHEN I LEAVE the office later, he follows me outside. "You haven't told anyone," he says. "So I guess you believe me now?"

"Of course I believe you. I overreacted."

"I'll say." Sam clears his throat. "Well, I thought about it later, and I can see how what I did might look suspicious."

"You're not mad?"

"I wish you could have just trusted me," he admits.

Yeah, me too. "Sorry."

Sam touches my arm. "But maybe it's not fair to ask for trust when we know for sure that there's a traitor among us. Someone we probably trust actually is turning over info to the police."

My gut aches, but I nod. "I know." The desire to tell Sam exactly how much I know begins to engulf me. Have I done the right thing, keeping silent? If Raheem stops turning over secrets, does it do any harm to keep what I know to myself?

"There was money in the envelope I took, but the man isn't a cop," Sam says. "He's a doctor."

"A doctor?" I claw my way out of my anguish, try to pay closer attention. "What kind of doctor?"

"Doesn't matter," Sam says. "He has a nice office downtown and his patients are a bunch of rich old white people. He has a lot of money and he donates to our clinic once a month. I was there to get this month's money."

"Why doesn't he mail it in like everyone else?"

"You don't mail wads of cash," Sam says. "And he doesn't want anyone to know he gives us money. He's afraid he'll lose his clients. So I go to pick it up."

"I saw him outside the clinic before," I say. "I guess that makes sense now."

Sam nods. "He came down twice to see what the clinic looks like, to be sure it meets high medical standards. His money is helping us get better medicine and equipment."

"That's good." Except it makes me feel doubly guilty for doubting him. "I want to go home now." The words sound foreign coming from me.

His hand touches my arm. "Maxie, are you all right?"

"Fine. I'm sorry I jumped to conclusions."

Sam shrugs. "How could you ever have guessed the real thing? It's pretty weird."

"Yeah," I reply, slinking away.

CHAPTER 76

I NEED TO KNOW HOW YOU'RE SITTING WITH this," Raheem says first thing. What—is camping on the couch waiting for me his new job or something?

"Not good," I snap. "What do you think? How am I supposed to sit?"

"You're acting like it's the end of the world."

Can't he see how the world is ending? My world, the world I've wanted so badly to be a part of.

"Rocco's my friend. Slim is—" I sigh. "Cherry's heart is broken now. You know that?"

"They would have found out some other way. They always do. That's how the pigs stay on top."

"We're supposed to be opposite of them!" I cry.

"We are."

I glare at him through narrowed eyes.

"Maxie, what are you thinking?" he says. "What are you going to do?"

I cross my arms. "I haven't told anybody, if that's what you mean."

"Maxie—"

"Is it over?" I interrupt.

Silence. Then, "We can get by for quite a while on the cash they already gave me. I don't want you worrying about any of this."

I stalk toward the bedroom, trying to ignore the fact that he didn't actually answer the question.

CHAPTER 77

I CROSS THROUGH THE BACK ROOM OF THE OFFICE, toward the kitchen. Leroy and Hamlin have their heads close together. As usual I'm invisible to them.

"It follows," Leroy's saying. "I spoke to Rocco inside, and he says only those four guys knew for sure where they'd be meeting that day."

My feet keep moving, but my heart stalls. In the kitchen, I hover near the doorway, listening closely.

"Let's have a conversation with him. See if we can shake anything loose."

"He's coming in for a policing shift after he gets off work this afternoon."

I lean against the doorjamb. I don't know whether to be nervous or relieved. If Leroy figures out on his own it was Raheem, then the truth is out there and I'm off the hook.

"Seems out of character for him, though, doesn't it?" Leroy says.

"How do you know? We haven't known him that long."
But, no, Leroy's known Raheem forever. Something's
wrong here.

"We haven't known a lot of these people long. That
doesn't necessarily mean . . ."

Hamlin sighs. "Look we're not going to accuse him,
okay? Let's just keep a close eye on Gumbo for a while."

I gasp. Slap my hand over my mouth to try and cover it.
I don't think they heard, because then Leroy says, "We can't
take our time with it, though. The policers are more and
more nervous every time they go out. They're all second-
guessing each other. It's getting out of control, and how long
before folks take matters into their own hands?"

"Gumbo's bearing the brunt of it. No one wants to go
on patrol with him," Hamlin says.

"Makes sense to me."

"But by the same logic, it could have been Raheem."

"Come on," Leroy scoffs. "We grew up together. It had
to be Gumbo, or else the pool is wider than we think. And
that's a whole new set of problems."

I back farther into the kitchen. Run the water in the sink
to drown out their voices. I hate what's happening here. The
unconditional trust in Leroy's voice when Raheem's name
came up. He's the perfect informant, I realize, because
everyone does trust him. No one would ever guess they

need to hold secrets from him. And now Leroy suspects Gumbo. Someone is going to be wrongfully accused. Someone is going to be held accountable for Raheem's mistakes. Can I stand by and let that happen?

I bend my head over the sink and drink water from the tap as a distraction. It doesn't especially work. I shut off the tap and wipe my mouth with my hand. I walk straight out into the room, straight up to Hamlin and Leroy. No idea what I'm going to do when I get there.

"Hey, Maxie-girl," Leroy says. "How are my eyes and ears?" I hear the teasing humor in his voice and I know it means he doesn't take me seriously. Never has. Never will. He doesn't expect me to come back with any real information, because the information I've already given him is flawed. Surely Leroy knows by now that the man in the car outside the clinic is a doctor. Sam's friend. But he never told me I was wrong. He let me go on believing I had reported a spy. Let me go on believing that I was making a difference.

"How are my eyes and ears?" If he had said it any other way, I might have been able to hold it in. I might have been able to put it off another day, another week, maybe forever. But as it is, the truth is bursting out of me. I have information. I have knowledge that can help. Finally, what I can do actually matters. Right now I can make my mark as the girl who discovered the traitor in the ranks. I can save the Pan-

thers from wondering who it is that doesn't have our backs, and maybe save Gumbo or someone else from accusation or a punishment he doesn't deserve.

But to speak means to sacrifice something, something so special between me and my brother. It would destroy him, destroy us, and I can see it all unfolding and turning ugly in front of my eyes.

"Can you excuse us, Maxie?" Hamlin says. "We need to speak in private." Five seconds ago, I was listening to everything, and they didn't even notice. Now that they do see me, they want to send me away. I can't win.

I can't stand to be here any longer. I can't stand to be that girl everyone laughs at, the one who wants to be a Panther so bad she bleeds it and they still say no. I'm tempted to run, to hide my face and hide the truth a while longer. But I don't move a single inch. I stand and let myself cry in front of them, because I know how it feels to run. I know how it feels to hide. And the thing with the Panthers is supposed to be about putting all that behind us and standing up.

"Maxie?" Leroy says, suddenly concerned.

"I know who the informant is." The words all but slice my throat coming out.

I've told them before, many times, that I know what being a Panther means. I know what you have to give up.

I was wrong. I didn't know, not everything. Not enough. I thought it always meant giving up your life, being willing to die for the people, for the cause, but apparently sometimes it means doing something that's hard to live with. Like taking someone's life, with a bullet or with your words. Sometimes it means harboring a wound that can't be seen, one that bleeds on the inside with no hope of stopping. Ever.

CHAPTER 78

WHEN I COME INTO OUR ROOM, Raheem is lying on the bed, arms crossed beneath his head, staring out the window.

"You told them." He says it like it was inevitable somehow, and maybe it was.

I nod.

He rolls to his feet with a sigh. "Okay, then."

"Not okay," I blurt. "Everything's ruined! They're never going to trust me again."

Raheem scoffs. "Well, you got bigger problems now, kid." He reaches under the bed and pulls out a big green duffel bag. Spreads it on the mattress.

I sink onto the bed. Everything we've worked for, destroyed. "How could you do this to me?"

"Why do you think I did this in the first place?" he shouts. "I did it for you."

"We coulda got by," I shout back. "We always did before."

"Yeah, well, we weren't getting by. Not this time."

"I'd rather starve than be a traitor."

Raheem towers over me, glistening with rage, with tears. "You don't know what it means to starve. Not like Mama. Not like me." His voice cracks. "We always put you first."

He rips through the closet, tossing stuff onto the bed. He starts shoving it all into the duffel.

It dawns on me, finally, what he's doing. He's packing. "Where are you going?"

"Anywhere but here."

"You're leaving?"

"Jesus, Maxie. Did you think I was joking when I said they would kill me?"

"No, but . . ." I try to fathom it. The Panthers aren't about killing people, we just want to protect the community. "Leroy wouldn't do that."

"Okay, fine," he says. "Maybe not Leroy. Maybe not tomorrow. But someone, someday, with a trigger itch and a grudge. Probably someday soon."

"No." I fight it. The truth of it.

"And I'd deserve it, too," he says bitterly. "After what I did. Do you think I didn't hate it? That I don't hate myself for doing it?" He sighs. "Every moment in those pigs' presence, every little thing I told them, knowing how they'd use it?"

The bed seems to sag beneath me. "So you're leaving."

"Getting as far from Chicago as I can."

"Oh." I can't bring myself to say it: *What are we going to do without you?* "For how long?"

Raheem chokes on a laugh. "You better hope that job comes through for Ma; otherwise you're going to have to go and get something yourself. Someone's got to bring money in. You'll see how it is, and then you come back again and judge me."

The sound of the duffel zipper is the sound of something being sliced, torn, ruined. Raheem hefts the bag in his hand, testing the weight. Sets it back down. He looks around the room wearing this distant expression, like a part of him is already long gone.

"Okay," he says quietly. All the mad that was in him seems to have softened. "Come give me a hug before I go. I don't know when we'll see each other."

Tears spring to my eyes. I don't like the sound of that. "Heem," I whisper.

"It's okay," he says. "Just get over here. I gotta go."

My arms lock around his waist and he holds the back of my head with his big hand. I want to say I'm sorry, and I am, but it doesn't seem like enough.

"Are you going to hate me forever?" I whisper. Half of me thinks it was all wrong, what I did.

Raheem sighs. I feel his breath, his head bent over mine. "You do what you have to do, right? And afterward, you figure out how to live with it."

CHAPTER 79

WHEN I GO LOOKING FOR SAM, it's because I want him to hold me and tell me everything is going to be all right. My eyes stream with tears. I don't bother to stem them. The terror of what I've done seems to be hiding around every corner, leaping out.

"Raheem is the traitor," I tell him. No way to ease into it.

Sam knows already, has been looking for me, too. "I heard." He opens his arms to me. "I can't believe it."

I cry against his chest and he tightens his arms around me. "We're going to figure it out," he says. "We're going to get through it." He's hurt too. Betrayed. Like we all are. It's in the very air: *Raheem, how could you?*

"How'd they catch him?" Sam says. "How long has it been going on?"

"What?" I lift my head. He's looking at me, open wondering on his face. He knows, but he doesn't know everything. Maybe Hamlin and Leroy kept the source of the news to themselves.

"I—I had to tell them," I manage, through the fist my throat has become. "It was wrong, all wrong, what he was doing."

Sam draws back, holding me at arm's length.

"You turned him in?" He says it like he can't believe it. I can't believe it myself. "How could you do that?" He releases me like I'm radioactive.

"Please," I beg, reaching out a hand to him. I don't want to talk it through, I just want Sam to make me feel better. He steps away from my touch as if it'll burn him. As if the traitor bug is contagious. Raheem betrays the Panthers. I betray Raheem. Which is worse, in the end?

"You didn't tell on me when you thought it was me," Sam says. "That's your brother!"

"I know," I cry.

Sam looks dangerously close to tears himself. "You never turn your back on family."

"The Panthers are family, too," I whisper.

"No," he says. "No."

"I did what I had to," I say. "Power to the people."

Sam looks at me coldly. "I don't even know who you are anymore."

Then he walks away.

CHAPTER 80

I T TAKES EVERY PIECE OF COURAGE INSIDE OF me to walk into the Panther office and face Leroy and Jolene. I do it, but everything from my stomach to my fingertips is trembling.

"Raheem left town," I tell them. "You don't have to worry about him anymore."

"He's gone?" Leroy says.

"I told him I had to tell you, so he left. That's everything I know. Please don't kill me."

"Honey, no," Jolene says. "You've been so brave." She comes around and hugs me. She's all soft and warm and I fade into her like a shadow. She brushes the side of my face.

"I don't know why he did it," I admit. I can't understand it, still. We needed money, but we've had hard times before. Hungry times. Times without power and washing laundry in the sink by hand. It hurts but we get through it.

I struggle not to cry against Jolene. I can't imagine betraying the Panthers, and Raheem has taught me everything I know. Does that mean I have what it takes to be a traitor inside me? I guess I must, because I've already turned traitor—against Raheem.

"People make mistakes for lots of reasons," Leroy says. "I think I can guess Raheem's."

"It's over now." Jolene's voice is reassuring, but through my squinted eyes I see Leroy shaking his head at her.

It's not over. Rocco and Slim are in prison. Fred Hampton's office has been raided. Who knows what else happened that we don't even know about. All because Raheem slipped information to the pigs.

And I'm caught up in it. By blood. And by the fact that I've shown myself as someone who knows how to betray.

I pull away from Jolene. "I'll leave now, if you want me to," I offer, knowing that I have to. Maybe the Panthers can't trust me again after this mess. It will break me, if they send me to the street, if my time in the Panther world is over, but I try to bury that knowledge deeper.

It's quiet for a moment. Long enough that I wonder if they're even going to speak, or if I'm just supposed to *know* it's time to walk away.

"Maxie, I still want you keeping your eyes out," Leroy

says. "There are always going to be people trying to bring us down."

"I can stay?" I whisper.

Jolene touches my face. "Maxie, everyone knows you're a Panther through and through."

CHAPTER 81

A PANTHER THROUGH AND THROUGH. It's what I've wanted. It's been everything. If she'd said it to me a week ago, a month ago, I would have been over the moon.

Even now I cling to it. Tell myself I did the right thing.

It's only been a day, but already I miss Raheem. I don't know how to think about him now, without a place to put him, like the bed across the room or policing the streets with the Panthers. I imagine him floating, getting smaller and smaller as he moves away and away.

I sit at the base of the wall, knees drawn up tight. The sweat that stings my skin doesn't quite jive with the fresh spring air. My pulse pumps beneath the skin of my throat like the flawed and ticking surface of an old forgotten clock. People come up, speak to me, but I'm locked here, unable to listen or respond.

I breathe toward a place in me that cannot be touched. I know I'm going to carry the weight of guilt for the rest of my days. Things I've heard, things people have said, do not sink in. *"It's not your fault. You did the right thing. Power to the people."* Every attempt at forgiveness crashes like an ocean wave, never fading, just lulling to rise again. Over and over. Crashing. The sound and the clean mist spray, but I'm nowhere near the water. I can never be clean of this.

To live for the people, to die for the people. What about the in-between? What happens between the moment you decide to give up your life and the moment you actually die? It feels like suspended animation, this call to arms. Unceasing. I can't begin to say I'm sorry. I can't begin to believe there was a right thing to do, a way to play both sides against the middle.

I start to see Raheem's betrayal as a betrayal not just of the Panthers but of me. Everything I've worked for dashed with a sweep of his hand into the pigs' enormous till. I can't forgive him. He won't forgive me, either, and I can't forgive myself. It's a wash of anguish.

Perhaps that's what it means to be a Panther in the end. To do the unforgivable. Willingly, without flinching. The greater good is worth our sacrifice. Worth more than one life, more than my destruction from the inside out. The worst part is, it's Raheem who taught me that.

CHAPTER 82

THE FIRST CHECK COMES A MONTH LATER, made out in my name. I've never had my own check before. It takes me a while to work out what it is. When I do, I want to tear it to shreds. Don't want to live off the government anymore, off the pigs.

Instead I hold the envelope in my hand, sit on the edge of the bed, and cry. Raheem found a new way to sell out, and he did it for me. To take care of me, make sure I can eat like a person and dress like a Panther really should. He did it all for me. And I sold him up the river. Across the ocean, as it turns out. To a place called Vietnam. A place where people die, and maybe there are even real live panthers stalking the jungle.

"Raheem enlisted," I tell Mama. "He's in the army now, headed to Vietnam."

"That's from him?" she asks, looking at the letter in my hand.

"Yeah," I lie. Let her think he's writing us direct, that it's more than his soldier's family stipend coming our way, that the words on the page are really from him and not generated by anonymous fingers in a typing pool someplace. "He says not to worry, and he promises we'll be taken care of."

C H A P T E R **8 3**

I SIT ON THE WALL, WATCHING EMMALEE AND Jimmy holding hands on a bench at the other side of the playground. Patrice is nowhere to be found. I don't even know what she's doing with herself these days. So much has changed.

Sam rolls through, in his leather jacket with the tape just so, like usual. I get it now. Because I long to wear the jacket Raheem gave me, to hold a piece of him close in case I never can again.

Sam turns my way. He's distant from me now, even as he approaches with a look on his face like it's time to talk at last. We've become buoys in the tide, sometimes drifting close, sometimes farther apart.

"Hi," he says.

"Hi, Sam."

"How are you?" he says, and I know he really cares.

"I don't know," I say. But I do know. I'm a Panther. Finally. "Okay, I guess."

"Stop blaming yourself," he says. "Raheem did what he did, and it's all on him."

"I know."

"Do you?" Sam crosses his arms, resting them on the wall beside me. Not exactly looking at me, like he's thinking out loud, and I just happen to be there. "The thing is, it's hard for me to imagine doing, you know"—he pauses—"what you did."

"You wouldn't have, would you?" But the picture is so not the same.

Sam rests his chin on his arms. "I don't know," he says. "That's the whole thing."

"You wouldn't have." Sam thinks before he acts, before he speaks. He would have seen past the moment, to everything that was going to come after. Nine times out of ten, I wish I hadn't done it. The last thing Raheem said keeps coming back to me: *You do what you have to do, and then you learn how to live with it.* It bugs me, because I don't know if he was talking about me, or himself, or both.

I look at Sam, in his jacket with the tape. I guess we all have stuff we have to live with, whether it was ever in our hands or not.

fireinthestreets

Here's the worst part. Raheem always wanted me to believe in him. He made all these promises, that he could take care of us and that I didn't have to worry. But I never could trust it, not all the way. I couldn't give him everything, the way he gave up everything for me. I gave up everything for something else. The Panthers are what I believe in.

CHAPTER 84

LEROY ENTERS THE OFFICE. EVERYONE breathes in as if to speak, starts hurrying toward him with news, questions, updates. But then no one says anything at all. The solemn look on his face freezes everything, leaves it all hanging unsaid in the air above us.

"Bad news," he says.

We hold our breaths, waiting for whatever it is to drop.

"Bobby Seale's been indicted. He's charged with conspiracy to incite the riots during the convention last summer."

Everyone groans.

"They're really blaming all that on us?" Lester says. "We were barely even there."

"Not entirely," Leroy says. "Bobby's one of eight who've been charged. The others are white guys from the anti-war movement."

"It was a white protest," Hamlin says. "No way to spin it any other way."

"They're saying Bobby's speeches helped inflame the crowd."

"That's a load of hogwash," Gumbo blurts out. "We were the only ones there not trying to start something."

The mood in the room is sizzling. Tense. Everyone's struggling to take in the news; I'm struggling with it myself.

"We're going to take care of this," Leroy declares. "I just wanted everyone to be informed." His face drawn tight, he retreats to the rear room.

"Bobby was barely at the convention," Emmalee says. "They think he caused the riots?" We're sprawled on the floor in the back room, where Little Betty's play pad is set up. It's just a blanket on the floor ringed in with boxes so she can't crawl all over the room, now that she's started trying to do that. Emmalee lies on her back inside the circle.

"It's stupid," I tell her. "They're just out to get him." I'm sitting on the boxes, letting Little Betty hold my fingers as she pulls herself up and tries to balance. Her short legs wobble, and one after the other she sort of waves her chubby feet; it's like she knows they're supposed to take her somewhere, but she can't quite make it happen yet. She's growing. She grins up at me with her two tiny front teeth.

We don't have that many photographs at home, but we have one of me with two front teeth, and we have one of Raheem a little bit older that was probably taken at the same time. Now Mama gets the pictures out most days. She sits with Raheem's picture and cries. I haven't told her the truth of why he left, just that Raheem is doing what he has to. For us. She can't understand why he didn't say a real good-bye, and I have no answers.

"Why did it take so long for this to happen?" Emmalee wonders. "The convention was months ago."

I'm only partly thinking about Bobby's case. My mind is going in all different directions. "Um, Leroy said the grand jury had to review the facts and decide if there was enough evidence to have a trial. Apparently that takes a long time sometimes. I think it's weird too." I feel proud to know the answer to her question. Usually Emmalee is the one who knows it all.

Little Betty places her fat feet on top of mine. Grins. Those two teeth can just break your heart. If it isn't already broken.

Jolene comes by and scoops up the baby. She cuddles and kisses her. I look away while it happens. It's just too sweet.

"Maxie, I want you here this afternoon," Jolene says. "Bobby Seale's lawyers are coming by and we need some people to sit in. Listen to what they're planning and what they need from us."

"Me?"

"Yes," Jolene says. "We'll be helping them with any research we can in preparation for the trial. Maybe reviewing notes and paperwork. I'm not sure what all. We'll find out this afternoon."

"You want me?" It doesn't really register. The sole thought in my head is that I have to get better at reading.

"You'll be great," Jolene says. She brushes the hair away from my face as she sometimes does. The touch makes me realize how bad I want her to go ahead and hug me, the way Mama won't do anymore now that worry over Raheem has driven her closer to the edge.

"Really? You think so?"

Jolene rests a hand on my shoulder. "Someone was always telling me you ought to be a lawyer." Her soft tone holds no bitterness, even though the only someone who would ever say something like that has got to be Raheem.

"Don't you want some firsthand experience?" Jolene says. I've been quiet too long.

I sit up straighter. This is my chance.

"You'll have to alternate it with school and PE classes and your weapons training," she continues. "So it'll be a lot of work."

My mind snaps into focus. "Weapons training?"

Jolene smiles. "It's about time, don't you think?"

"Yes." My eyes tear up. "I want to do it. Thank you for picking me."

"We'll see you tomorrow morning. Six a.m., for the lineup," she says, walking away.

For a while I'm just sitting there, gazing at the sandbags up against the windows. Thinking about things like bullets. Tiny pieces of flying metal. Broken shards of glass. Thinking about things like secrets. Bits of information, floating in the ether. Thinking about how one thing leads to another, and every day there are new bullets, new shards. New things to watch out for.

But it's happening. Everything I dreamed of, though not at all in the way I dreamed it. Maxie Brown, Black Panther.

I feel a hand on my shoulder. "Come outside with me," Sam says. "I just heard."

He leads me out to the sidewalk, just beyond the sandbagged windows.

"Congratulations," he says. Grinning, he breaks into a little refrain: "For she's a jolly good Panther, for she's a jolly good Panther."

I smile. Not so much at the song but at the fact that he's

singing. Making a joke. It has been a while since things felt
light between us. I kiss him on the cheek. Can't help it. He's
so darn cute.

"I have something for you," he tells me. He has a small
paper bag with him.

"Is it mittens?" I tease, reminding him of the first gift he
ever gave me, back when he was trying to win my heart. He
won that particular battle a long while ago, but I can't say
I lost in the process.

His face remains semiserious.

"What, then?"

He opens the bag and lets me look inside. I blink at the
contents, confused. "It's Raheem's," Sam says. "Before he
left he made me promise to keep it for you." He tips the bag,
bringing the object nearer to the opening. Not revealing it
to the whole street, but just to me.

I stare at the silver handgun resting against Sam's palm.
Raheem's gun. Handed down to me.

"He said to give it to you when you seemed ready. Do
you feel ready?" Sam says uncertainly.

It's everything I've wanted. Everything my whole life
has been building toward. A way to make sense of it all, a
way to do something. I'm thinking ahead, toward the six
a.m. lineup and how loud I'm going to shout when Leroy
says "Who we gonna be? How we gonna live?"

"The Black Panther Party. Gonna live for the people." I practice it in my mind, like I've done a thousand times. It makes me excited, gives me the first inkling of happiness I've had since I found Raheem in that alley.

Raheem is ever present in my mind. He always finds ways to look out for me, even from a distance. I suppose he means to be passing a torch to me, and I wonder if he's really never coming back. If he can feel me from a distance, the way I feel him—in my memory and in my heart—I know I will make him proud.

"Maxie?"

Sam watches me carefully. I smile at him. My fingers fold around the edges of the bag, taking back what is rightfully mine. Maybe it's always been mine, I just needed to reach out and take it.

"Yes," I tell him. "I was born ready."

ACKNOWLEDGMENTS

THANK YOU, AS ALWAYS, TO MY PARENTS and my brother, Kobi, as well as to all my family and friends who continuously support my work.

Thank you to my many writer friends who read early drafts and sections of this book and offered ever-wise advice: Laurie Calkhoven, Josanne La Valley, Marianna Baer, Elizabeth Bird, Donna Freitas, Marie Rutkoski, Jill Santopolo, Eliot Schrefer, Susan Amessé, Holly Kowitt, Catherine Stine, Peter Havholm, Edith Kunhardt Davis, Caroline Nastro, Lindsey Tate, and Kerri Topping.

Thanks to Tangi for her double Dutch notes; to my mom for being a stellar research assistant, investigating random historical details; and to Pam Harkins and Seth Harkins for sharing memories of Chicago in '68 and the Democratic National Convention. Numerous adult readers of *The Rock and the River* have also shared their memories of this time with me, and I am grateful for the ways you all have helped me open the door to this history.

Thank you to my agent, Michelle Humphrey, and to my editorial and publishing team at Aladdin/Simon & Schuster—especially Fiona Simpson, Liesa Abrams, Mara Anastas, Kate Angelella, Laura Antonacci, Annie Berger, Bethany Buck, Michelle Fadlalla, Anna McKean, Karin Paprocki, and Catharine Sotzing—and to everyone else at Aladdin whose work has supported my previous books and helped bring this book to fruition.

This book would not exist at all without the many other people who helped its companion, *The Rock and the River*, achieve the success it has. Thanks especially to the dozens of librarians and bloggers who spread the word about the book—those wonderful early reviews and shout-outs made all the difference. I'm forever grateful to the 2010 Coretta Scott King Book Award Jury for honoring me with the CSK/John Steptoe Award for New Talent, and to the NAACP Image Awards selection committee who chose *The Rock and the River* as an Image Awards nominee for Outstanding Literary Work for Youth/Teens.

Finally, thank you to the many readers of *The Rock and the River* who were excited enough about this world and these characters to ask, "What happened next?" Well now you know!

KEKLAMAGOON

has worked with youth-serving nonprofit organizations in New York and Chicago. She is now a full-time author and speaker. She holds an MFA in Writing for Children and Young Adults from the Vermont College of Fine Arts and a BA from Northwestern University. Kekla lives in New York City, and online at: keklamagoon.com.